'So…' Alessandro drawled, handing Laura a glass. 'Are you going to remain standing by the door like a sentry or are you going to sit down and say what you have to say?'

His fingers had brushed against hers, and every muscle and nerve in her body had reacted.

'You never mentioned how long you intend staying in Scotland…' She inched her way towards the table and sat down.

'Undecided. Why? Do I make you feel uncomfortable? I wouldn't want to put a spoke in the wheel, but…' He shrugged, sipped his drink and looked at her over the rim of his glass. 'Needs must.'

'What needs?'

'That's a somewhat leading question, wouldn't you say?'

If they were referring to *his* needs, then he might very well meet them by staying. Because suddenly he had a vivid image of her in his bed, sprawled in all her glorious, lush beauty, her delicate heart-shaped f̶a̶c̶e̶ ̶h̶e̶a̶t̶e̶d̶ with desir

Cathy Williams can remember reading Mills & Boon® books as a teenager, and now that she is writing them she remains an avid fan. For her, there is nothing like creating romantic stories and engaging plots, and each and every book is a new adventure. Cathy lives in London and her three daughters—Charlotte, Olivia and Emma—have always been and continue to be the greatest inspiration in her life.

Books by Cathy Williams

Mills & Boon® Modern™ Romance

At Her Boss's Pleasure
The Real Romero
The Uncompromising Italian
The Argentinian's Demand
Secrets of a Ruthless Tycoon
Enthralled by Moretti
His Temporary Mistress
A Deal with Di Capua
The Secret Casella Baby
The Notorious Gabriel Diaz
A Tempestuous Temptation

One Night With Consequences

Bound by the Billionaire's Baby

Seven Sexy Sins

To Sin with the Tycoon

Protecting His Legacy

The Secret Sinclair

Visit the author profile page at millsandboon.co.uk for more titles

A PAWN IN THE PLAYBOY'S GAME

BY
CATHY WILLIAMS

Published in Great Britain 2015
by Mills & Boon, an imprint of Harlequin (UK) Limited,
Eton House, 18-24 Paradise Road, Richmond, Surrey, TW9 1SR

© 2015 Cathy Williams

ISBN: 978-0-263-24906-4

Printed and bound in Spain
by CPI, Barcelona

A PAWN IN THE PLAYBOY'S GAME

To my three wonderful and inspiring daughters

CHAPTER ONE

'DON'T KNOW WHAT you're doing here.' Roberto Falcone glared at his son. He had shuffled to the front door and now he remained standing in front of it like a bouncer blocking entry to a club. 'Told you not to bother coming and meant it.'

Alessandro felt that familiar tension invade his body, the way it always did on those occasions when he was in his father's company. Usually, though, they at least managed pleasantries before he felt like spinning on his heel and walking as fast as he could in the opposite direction. This time, there was no polite surface small talk and Alessandro braced himself for an impossibly difficult weekend.

Which they would both have to endure because there was no choice.

'Are you going to let me in or are we going to have this conversation on the doorstep? Because if we are, I'll get my coat from the car. I'd rather not die from frostbite just yet.'

'You won't die from frostbite,' Roberto Falcone scoffed. 'It's practically tropical here.'

Alessandro didn't bother to argue. He'd had a lot of experience when it came to disagreeing with his father. Roberto Falcone might be eighty years old but there was nothing he gave up without a fight, and arguing about whether eight degrees Celsius counted as cold or not was just one of those things. He was a hardy soul who lived

in Scotland and thought that blizzard conditions were a
bracing challenge. Real men cleared snowdrifts half-naked
and barefoot! His son was a softie who lived in London
and switched on the central heating the second the sun
went behind a cloud.

And never the twain would meet.

Which was why duty visits were limited to three times
a year and lasted as long as it took for the limited well of
polite conversation to run dry.

Except this was more than a duty visit and he had
known that his father wasn't going to make things easy.

'I'll get my coat.'

'Don't bother. Now that you've landed here, I suppose
I don't have much choice but to let you in, but if you think
that I'm going to be heading down to London with you,
then you've got another think coming. I'm not budging.'

In the cold, gathering gloom, they stared at one another, Alessandro's expression veiled, his father's fiercely
determined.

'We'll discuss this when I'm inside,' Alessandro said.
'Why have you answered the door? Where's Fergus?'

'It's the weekend. Man deserves a break.'

'You had a stroke six months ago and you're still recovering from a fractured pelvis. The man's paid enough
to give up his breaks.'

Roberto scowled but Alessandro didn't back down.
Frankly, this wasn't the time for pussyfooting round the
issue. Like it or not, his father was going to return to London with him in three days' time. The contents of the house
could be packed up and shipped south once the place had
been vacated.

His mind was made up and once Alessandro had made
his mind up on anything, he was not open to discussion,
far less persuasion. His father could no longer cope with

the rolling Victorian mansion, even if he could afford an army of hired help if he chose. Neither could he cope with the acres of lawns and garden. He liked plants. Alessandro would introduce him to the marvels of Kew Gardens.

The brutal truth was that Roberto Falcone was now frail, whether he wanted to admit it or not, and he needed somewhere small, somewhere closer to Alessandro, somewhere in London.

'I'll get my bag,' Alessandro said abruptly. 'You go in and I'll join you in the sitting room. I take it you haven't dispatched *all* the help...because you felt they needed some time out from doing what they're so handsomely paid to do?'

'You might be lord of that manor of yours in London,' Roberto retorted, 'and I wouldn't think of questioning you if you chose to give whoever works for you a weekend off, but this is *my* manor and I can do whatever I want.'

'Let's not kick off this weekend on an argument,' Alessandro said heavily. He looked at the elderly man in front of him, still leonine in appearance with his thick head of steel-grey hair, his piercing dark eyes and his impressive height, at six foot one only a couple of inches shorter than him. The only hint of his frailty was the walking stick and, of course, a thick wad of medical notes residing in the hospital ten miles due west.

'Freya is here. There's food in the kitchen, which is where you will find me. Had I known you were going to descend on me, I might have asked her to prepare something a little less simple, but you're here now and salmon and potatoes is going to have to do.'

'You knew I was coming,' Alessandro pointed out patiently. A sharp gust of wind, carrying the sort of bitter cold rarely experienced in London, blew his dark hair away from his face. 'I emailed you.'

'Must have slipped my mind.'

Clenching his jaw in pure frustration, Alessandro watched as his father shuffled away, leaving the front door wide open.

The move to London was going to be a big step, for both of them. They barely had anything to say to one another. Lord only knew how more frequent meetings were going to play out, but there was no way he could continue making laborious trips to the depths of Scotland every time his father had a mishap, and there were no siblings with whom he could share the burden.

Just him. An only child shunted off to boarding school at the age of seven, returning back to their vast, cold mansion every holiday, where nannies and cooks and cleaners had picked up the role of parent because his father had rarely been in evidence, appearing only at the end of the day when they had dined at opposite ends of the formal dining table, waited on by the very people with whom Alessandro had spent his day.

Until, of course, he had become old enough to begin spending the occasional holidays with friends. His father had not once objected. Alessandro suspected that he had probably been quietly relieved. There was only so much polite conversation to be made across the length of a twenty-seat table.

The polite conversation was still made but at least now Alessandro could take it in his stride, at least he had stopped trying to find reasons behind his father's coldness, stopped wondering whether things might have been different had he remarried after the death of Muriel Falcone, stopped trying not to be a disappointment. That particular youthful sentiment had long disappeared.

Hitching his overnight bag over his shoulder and remotely locking his glossy black SUV, Alessandro decided that he would have to find some hobbies for his father the second he arrived in London.

Hobbies that would take him out of the luxurious three-bedroom ground-floor apartment in a small, portered Georgian block, which had been bought for him. A man with hobbies would be a happy man. Or at least a relatively invisible one. Too much visibility was not going to work for either of them.

Returning to Standeth House, for Alessandro, was like returning to a mausoleum. Same cold feel, although now that it would shortly be put on the market he found that he could better appreciate the impressive flagstoned hall-way and all the period features that he would never have dreamed of having in anywhere he personally owned but which, he conceded, had a certain something.

And, with as much money as you could fling a stick at, it had been well maintained. His father had been born into wealth, had maintained and increased it in his life-time and had not stinted when it came to spending it on his surroundings. He had always been generous financially if parsimonious when it came to everything else.

He found his father in the kitchen, where, despite what he had said, there was no housekeeper.

Alessandro frowned. 'You said Freya would be here to take care of the food.'

Roberto looked at his son from under grey, bushy brows. 'Left at four. Note on the cooker jogged my mem-ory. Forgot to mention it.' He ladled a generous portion of food onto his plate and went to the kitchen table, leav-ing Alessandro to help himself. 'Sick dog. Had to take it to the vet. It happens. And before you launch into a con-versation about how you've come here to tear me away from my house and my land, eat some food and talk about something else. Been months since you ventured up here.

You must have something to talk about aside from rescuing me from my old age.'

'Work's fine.' Alessandro looked at the slab of salmon on his plate with distaste. Freya was in her mid-sixties and had been his father's cook for the past fifteen years. She was as thin as a rake, only smiled on high days and bank holidays and would never be asked to cook for the queen. Or anyone with halfway decent tastebuds. Her productions were as spartan as she was. Potatoes, some vegetables and fish, which were unadorned with anything that could fall under the heading of tasty.

'I've added a niche publishing house to my portfolio, along with three small hotels on the other side of the Atlantic. It's a little comic relief from my IT companies and telecommunications.' He might have benefited from being the son of a wealthy man, might have been to the finest schools, been given the most pocket money, treated to the fastest car at an age when fast cars and young boys should never have had even a nodding acquaintance, but he had refused point-blank to show the slightest interest in his father's empire. When it came to earning a living, Alessandro had always known that he would go it without any help from his austere and distant parent.

Not that Roberto had asked. Until a decade ago he had still been running his empire himself.

Neither had Alessandro accepted any start-up money. He had used his brains to super-achieve at university and he had continued using his brains to super-achieve at everything that had followed. As far as he was concerned, the less he had to do with Roberto Falcone, the better. They maintained contact, paid lip service to their relationship, and that was that. It worked.

'And still chasing the same idiots you were chasing when I last saw you? What was the name of that one you dragged up here? Acted as though she didn't recognise what mud was and refused to go near the garden because it had rained and her high heels couldn't take the strain.' Roberto guffawed.

'Sophia,' Alessandro said through gritted teeth. This was the first time his father had come right out and voiced his scathing disapproval of the women he had met in the past, girlfriends Alessandro had taken with him because a third party, even an intellectually challenged third party, was worth her weight in gold when it came to smoothing over pregnant pauses.

And it had to be said that the women he dated more than made up for their sometimes limited conversation with their looks. He liked them leggy, long-haired, slender and outrageously good-looking. The size of their IQs didn't really come into it. Just as long as they pleased him, looked good, said yes when he wanted them to say yes and didn't get attached.

'Sophia…that's the one. Nice-looking girl with all that bouncy hair but difficult to have a conversation with. I'm guessing that doesn't bother you, though. Where is she now?' He looked around him as though suddenly alert to the possibility that the six-foot-tall brunette might be hiding behind the kitchen door or underneath the counter.

'It didn't work out.' The gloves were certainly off if his father was diving into his personal life. Polite was beginning to look like a cosy walk in the park in comparison. Was this how Roberto intended to retaliate to the winds of change? By getting too close to the bone for comfort?

'Reason I brought that up…' Roberto finished his salmon and shoved the plate to one side '…is if that's the kind of people who hang around the rich in that city of yours, then it's just another reason why I won't be joining you. So you can start looking for tenants for that apartment you bought.'

'There are lots of different kinds of people in London.' And who, exactly, were his father's friends here anyway? He'd met one or two couples, bumped into them while out to dinner locally with his father over the years, but how often did he mix with them?

Like vast swathes of his father's life, that was just another mystery. For all Alessandro knew, his father could be cooped up in his country estate from dawn till dusk with nothing but the hired help and his plants for company.

He had long trained himself to feel no curiosity. The door had been shut on him a long time ago and it wasn't going to reopen.

'And some of them might have more to talk about than the weather, the tidal changes and salmon fishing. On another note, I see Freya is continuing to shine as a cordon bleu chef...'

'Simple food for a simple man,' Roberto returned coldly. 'If I wanted anything fancier, I would have employed one of those TV chef types who have fish restaurants in Devon and use ingredients nobody's ever heard of.'

For the first time in living memory, Alessandro felt his lips twitch with amusement at his father's asperity.

But then he reminded himself that humour wasn't behind this conversation. These were all little warning jabs before the real battle began in the morning.

He stood up, irritated that on a Friday evening there was no one around to at least clear the table. Alessandro didn't have anyone working for him, aside from a cleaner three times a week and his driver, but if he had he would have damned well made sure that they were available to work when he needed them, instead of skipping off to give their dog cuddles and cough syrup.

'I have some work to get through by ten tonight.' He

looked at his watch and then at his father, who had not moved a muscle to stand up.

'No one's keeping you.' Roberto fluttered his hand in the general direction of the kitchen door.

'Heading up to bed now?'

'Maybe not. Maybe I should have a late-night walk through the grounds so that I can appreciate the open space before you start manhandling me into a flat in that city of yours.'

'Freya in tomorrow? Or will her dog still require her urgent attention?' Alessandro wasn't going to be provoked into a simmering argument that he would take to bed with him. 'Because if she plans on spending the weekend with her sick dog, I'll head into town first thing in the morning and stockpile some food that's easy to cook.' He stood up and began clearing the table. 'Just enough to last the weekend,' he threw over his shoulder.

'Don't need you cooking for me. Perfectly capable of throwing something in a pan.'

'It's not a problem.'

'If she doesn't come, she might send someone in her place. Sometimes does that.'

'How reliable *is* this bloody woman?' Alessandro turned to his father's face and scowled. 'I had a look at the accounts the last time I was here, and she's paid a fortune! Are you telling me that she skives off when she feels like it?'

'I'm telling you that it's *my* money and I'll spend it any damn way I want to! If I want to pay the woman to show up every other weekend and dance on the table, that's *my* shout!'

Alessandro looked at his father narrowly and eventually shrugged.

'If she doesn't show up,' Roberto inserted grudgingly, 'she'll send someone in her place.'

'Fine. In that case, I'll leave all the dirty dishes so that she or her replacement has something to do when they get here. And now I'm heading off to do some work. I take it you won't be needing your study?'

'What would an old, feeble man with an old, feeble brain need a study for?' He waved his hand, dismissing Alessandro without sparing him a glance. 'It's all yours.'

Laura Reid finally hopped on her bike and headed out of the terraced house she shared with her grandmother forty-five minutes later than planned.

Things moved at a different speed here. She had now lived here for nearly a year and a half and she was still getting used to the change of pace. She wasn't sure whether she would ever completely get used to it.

On a bright, cold Saturday morning, her intentions might have been to start the day at the crack of dawn, get all the little chores done and dusted by nine and then cycle up to the big house, but intentions counted for nothing here.

People had dropped by. Her grandmother had taken herself off to Glasgow to visit her sister for two weeks and every well-wishing friend had popped around to make sure she was all right, as if her grandmother's absence might herald all sorts of untold disasters. Was she making sure to eat properly? Curious, concerned eyes peered into the kitchen in the hope of spotting a pie or two. Had she remembered that the garbage people had changed their collection day because old Euan's son had gone to hospital and his brother was covering?

Was she remembering to make sure the logs were kept dry? Edith would have a fit if she returned to find them soaked through and who knew what the weather would bring in the next ten days. And make sure to lock all the doors! Mildred had told Shona who had told Brian who had told his daughter Leigh that there had been a spate of petty thefts in the neighbouring village and you couldn't be too careful.

The wind on her face felt great as she began cycling away from the town.

It meant freedom and peace and was always a time when she replayed her life in slow motion in her head, the way it had turned full circle so that she was right back where she had started.

The young girl who had gaily gone to London to take up a position as PA to a CEO in an upwardly mobile, just-gone-public company was no more. At least now, when she thought of that time in her life, her mouth no longer filled with bitterness and despair. Instead, she could put it all in perspective and see her experiences as a valuable learning curve.

She had worked for a busy, aggressive company, which, coming from this small town, had been a first. She had seen the bright lights and felt the buzz of big-city excitement. She had hopped on the Underground and jostled with the crowds at rush hour. She had eaten on the run and gone to wine bars with new friends.

And two years into her bright, shiny life she had met a guy, someone so wildly different from every guy she had ever met that was it any wonder she had fallen hopelessly in love with him?

The only downside was that he had been her boss. Not *directly* her boss, but far, far higher than her in the company food chain, recently transferred back to London from New York.

And naive as she had been, all the warning signs that

would have been flagged up to any woman with just a bit more experience had passed her by.

Rich guy…top job…cute, with little dimples and floppy blond hair…thirty-four and single…

Laura had been over the moon. She hadn't minded the weekends he'd been unable to spend with her because he'd visited his ailing father in the New Forest area…hadn't cared that meals out had always been in small, dark places miles away from the city centre…hadn't really twigged when he'd told her that once an arrangement was made, it was set in cement…no need for her to call him and, besides, he was just one of those guys who hated long, rambling telephone conversations on mobiles.

'There's never a time when it's convenient!' he had joked teasingly. 'You're either in the supermarket, about to hand over your credit card…or on the Underground, hanging on to a strap for dear life…or about to step into the shower… Leave the calling to me!'

She had for nearly a year until she had seen him out, quite by chance, with a sandy-haired woman hanging on to his arm and a little toddler sucking a lollipop, twisting round from her pushchair to look at him.

So much for love. She'd fallen for a married guy, had fallen for surface charm and a clever way with words.

She had worked out her notice and left and now she was ninety-nine per cent convinced that it had all been for the best. Secretarial work hadn't been for her. The job had been buzzy and well paid but the teaching job she did now was much more emotionally rewarding.

Plus everyone had to have a learning curve. She would never make the mistake of even *looking twice* at any man who was out of her league. If it looked too good to be true, it probably was.

It was a dull, cloudy morning and she could feel icy fingers trying to wriggle through the layers of her clothes... the vest, jumper, padded sleeveless waterproof that bulked her up so that she looked like a beach ball in search of a stretch of sand.

When she glanced over her shoulder, the little town had been left behind and there was roaming, rambling countryside all around her, stretching as far as the eye could see.

She slowed down. There was no place on earth as beautiful as Scotland. No place where you could practically hear the silence and the small sounds of nature, living, breathing nature. This was where she had grown up. Not this precise spot in this exact town, but in a very similar small town not a million miles away. She had moved to live with her grandmother when her parents had died. She had been just seven at the time. She had adjusted over time to the loss of her parents and it had taken her a lot less time to adjust to life in this part of Scotland because the scenery was so familiar to her.

She crested a hill, on either side of which russets, browns and stark, naked fields, stripped bare of colour, filled her with a sense of freedom, and there, just ahead of her, she could see the entrance to the long drive that led up to Roberto's house.

She slowed down, took her time pedalling her way up the drive. She never tired of this familiar route. In summer it was stunning, vibrant with green, the trees bending over the drive. In winter the bare trees were equally impressive, stretching up like talons reaching for the clouds.

The unexpected sight of a black SUV brought her to a halt and she slowly began walking the bike towards the front door.

Surprises were rarely of the good kind and this was a surprise because Roberto seldom had visitors. At least, not ones that weren't of the local variety. He had friends in the village…her grandmother was very pally with him, somewhat more than pally, she suspected, and of course he went to the usual things arranged for older people because there was quite a thriving community in the village for the over-sixties, but strangers appearing out of nowhere…?

Which only left one possibility and that made her heart sink. She'd never met the son and, in fairness, Roberto didn't dwell on him very much but the little he had said had not left a good impression either with her or with her grandmother.

She rang the doorbell and waited, heart beating fast.

Inside the house, specifically inside the office to which he had retreated after a tense breakfast with his father that had achieved less than zero, if that was possible, Alessandro heard the sharp ring of the doorbell and cursed fluently under his breath.

The vanishing hired help had remained vanished. His father, who was hell-bent on not listening to common sense, had taken himself off to his massive greenhouse, where, he said, he could have more fruitful conversation with his plants. Alessandro's plan to buy some food and do something with it had changed. He had decided to take his father out for dinner in the town because if his father was in a restaurant, there was just so far he could go when it came to dodging the inevitable conversation.

He reached the front door and pulled it open, his mood already foul because he could see the word *wasted* stamped all over his weekend.

The girl standing in front of him, gripping the handlebars of a bike that looked like a relic from a different era, took him momentarily by surprise.

She was a short, round little thing with copper-coloured hair that had been dragged back into a ponytail and eyes…

The purest, greenest eyes he had ever seen.

'About time.'

'I beg your pardon?' Laura had been expecting Roberto to answer the door. Instead, finding herself staring up at the most beautiful man she had ever seen in her life, her breathing had become jerky and her pulse was all over the place.

This would be the son and he was nothing like the mental picture she'd had in her head.

Her mental picture had been of a pompous, puffed-up, frankly ugly little guy who had his nose stuck in the air and never ventured out of London if he could help it. He hardly showed his face in Scotland and when he did, Roberto was always subdued afterwards, as if recovering from a virus.

Unfortunately, the man staring down at her with a glacial expression was too disturbingly good-looking for anybody's good. He positively towered over her and every inch of his body was hard-packed muscle. The black, long-sleeved T-shirt lovingly advertised that, as did the faded, low slung black jeans.

'Finished staring?' he asked coolly, and Laura went bright red. 'Because if you are, you can come in, head directly to the kitchen and begin doing what you're paid to do.'

'Sorry?' Laura blinked and stared at him in bewilderment before remembering the way he had sneered at her for staring, which made her immediately shift her gaze to the ivy clambering up the wall behind him.

Alessandro didn't bother answering. Instead, he stepped to one side and headed to the kitchen, expecting her to follow him.

Laura stared at his departing back with mounting anger.

'I'd like to know what's going on,' she demanded, having flung her bike to the ground and sprinted in his wake.

'What's going on…' Alessandro turned to face her and spread his arms wide '…is a kitchen that needs tidying. Which is what you're paid to do. Correct me if I'm wrong.' He leaned against the granite counter and looked at the round little bundle poised resentfully by the door. No one liked being reprimanded, but needs must, he thought. 'I understand that Freya couldn't make it to work yesterday because her dog was feeling under the weather, but it beggars belief that she couldn't be bothered to send her replacement until today and it's even more astonishing that her replacement can't be bothered to turn up until after ten in the morning!'

Placid by nature, Laura was discovering that it was remarkably easy to go from cool to boiling in seconds. She folded her arms and glared at him. 'If the kitchen needed tidying, why didn't you tidy it yourself?'

'I'll pretend I just didn't hear that!'

'I'd like to see Roberto…'

'And why would that be?' Alessandro drawled silkily. He folded his arms and stared at her. 'You might be able to get past him with some fairy-tale sob story about not being able to do the job you're paid to do because the dog's cousin got a cold or the rain was falling in the wrong direction so you just couldn't make it on time, but I'm made of tougher stuff. You should have been here at eight, as far as I'm concerned, and your pay will be docked accordingly!' Not, in all events, that that was going to be much of a concern considering his father would be out of the house, if not this weekend, then certainly by the end of the month.

'Are you *threatening* me?'

'It's not a threat. It's a statement of fact and frankly you should consider yourself lucky that I don't sack you on the spot.'

'This is too much! Where is Roberto?'

'Roberto?' He couldn't remember Freya addressing his father by his first name. Eyes narrowed now on her flushed face, Alessandro slowly pushed himself away from the counter and strolled towards her.

Like a predator with prey in its sight, he circled her before coming to a stop right in front of her, arms still folded, and this time his expression was thoughtful.

'Interesting,' he mused softly.

'What? What's interesting?' Laura inched back a little because his presence was so suffocating. She worked out that it wasn't just to do with the fact that the man was sinfully, unfairly sexy. There was also something about him, something intangible that sent shivers racing up and down her spine.

'Interesting that the hired help is now on a first-name basis with my father, who is a very rich man indeed.'

'I'm not following you.'

'Young girl…reasonably attractive…elderly man…loaded… I'm doing the maths and not liking the solution to the conundrum.'

Blood leached out of her face and there was a roaring in her ears. 'Are you accusing me of…of…of…?'

'I know. Incomprehensible, isn't it? My father is pushing eighty, has more money than he knows what to do with, and a whippersnapper who couldn't be more than… what?…twenty-two addresses him by his first name and seems pretty desperate to see him because, presumably, you know he'll rescue you from an uncomfortable situation. Smacks of unhealthy cosiness but, then, maybe I'm just being unfairly cynical.'

'Twenty-six, actually. I'm twenty-six.' A gold-digger? Was that what she was being accused of? A *reasonably attractive* gold-digger? Could there be any more insults stashed up his sleeve?

'Twenty-two…twenty-six. Doesn't really make much of a difference. You're still young enough to be his grand-daughter. Thank God I've come along and seen for myself what goes on here.'

'And I'm not the hired help.'

'No?' Alessandro's eyebrows shot up. Hired help or no hired help, the woman was still an opportunist, although he had to admit that the old man had reasonably good taste. Up close, her eyes were even more amazing, her skin sat-iny smooth with a sprinkling of freckles across the bridge of her nose, and her mouth…

His eyes dipped lazily to her mouth, which was full and perfectly shaped.

She might not be a model but she certainly wasn't a woman you would throw out of your bed on a rainy night.

She was fresh-faced and that in itself was oddly appeal-ing. No wonder she had managed to inveigle herself into his father's good graces. God knew how much she had managed to con out of him thus far.

'No!' Her skin burned under his scrutiny but she main-tained eye contact, even though every nerve in her body was reacting with tight hostility to his accusations.

'So who are you?'

'I'm Laura. I'm a friend. As you would discover if you went and got him!'

'Oh, I'll get him,' Alessandro said in a voice that made her teeth snap together in impotent fury. 'Just as soon as you and I have had a nice little chat. So why don't you have a seat at the table, *Laura*, and we'll…how do I put this?… get to know one another… No, wrong choice of words. *I'll* get to know *you* and *you'll* get to understand where *I'm* coming from.'

He smiled and she stared back angrily at him because

chilling though the smile was it was still horribly, horribly sexy.

'Fine,' she snapped, because if *he* wanted to have a word with her, he'd find that she had a few words of her own to share. She stalked off towards the kitchen table and in one easy movement yanked off the annoying waterproof and turned to face him with a toss of her head. 'And then I want to see your father.'

CHAPTER TWO

'YOU KNOW WHO I AM.' This was getting better and better. He had no idea who she was and yet she knew who he was. If she was a *friend*, then she was a *special* one, because he knew his father and one thing was for sure—Roberto Falcone was tight-lipped when it came to conversation. He was a man, and had always been a man, who spoke only when the situation demanded speech.

Alessandro could remember many a meal consumed in silence once the formalities of polite conversation had been exhausted.

'Of course I know who you are. Why wouldn't I? You're Alessandro, the son who never comes up to Scotland if he can help it.'

Alessandro flushed darkly. 'My father said that?'

'He didn't have to. You import your father down to London when you want to see him because it's easier. When was the last time you were here anyway?'

'How do you know my father?' Alessandro asked abruptly, cutting short any attempts to try to derail the conversation. So she wasn't the hired help and he should have recognised that from the get-go. Hired help didn't look like her and they certainly didn't have that stubborn tilt to their heads. His eyes roved over a body that, now that it was divested of the bulky parka, was rounded in all the right places. Small, voluptuous and...especially when

you combined it with her fresh-faced, make-up-free look…
downright sexy.

He sat down at the opposite end of the table. The
kitchen was one of the few really informal places in the
splendid mansion and Alessandro had never ceased to be
amazed that his father had given the go-ahead for it to be
furnished with weathered pine, a softly upholstered sofa
to the side, an oven that was well-worn and distressed
cupboards. Not at all a reflection of the stern, tight-lipped
man he was.

'I'm not here for an inquisition. I don't have to answer
your questions. Where is he? I came to ask whether there
was anything he needed from the shops. I didn't expect
to find you here.'

Alessandro found pretty much everything she said
highly offensive, from the tone of her voice to her refusal to
answer his questions to the implication that he was somehow vaguely responsible for his father's non-appearance.
Did she think that he had stashed Roberto away in a cupboard somewhere? To be retrieved a little later when it
suited him?

'And furthermore,' Laura added for good measure, 'I
resent your insinuation that because I'm young I'm only
friends with your father because he's rich. You have no
right to accuse me of something like that. You don't even
know who I am!' She leaned forward, her cheeks flushed,
more angry than she had ever been in her life. Angrier, it
felt, than when she had discovered that the so-called love
of her life was a married man with a toddler. Every single
thing about the arrogant man staring at her with forbidding
iciness got under her skin and made her see red.

'Frankly, I don't really care whether you resent my in-
sinuations or not,' Alessandro said coolly. 'I intend to protect my father's interests and if that means seeing off *a*

friend, then so be it. Answer my questions and we can move forward. Sit there foaming at the mouth…and back on your bike you go.'

'I am *not* foaming at the mouth!'

'How long have you known my father?'

Frustrated, Laura yanked her hair out of its constricting ponytail and ran her fingers through its thick length, and for a few seconds the air was sucked out of his lungs. It was a rich mane of colour and very long, longer than fashionably chic, cascading over her shoulders. He tore his eyes away and frowned, unsettled.

'Off and on for years.' Laura reluctantly gave him the information he wanted because she had a feeling that he wouldn't stop until she had told him what he wanted to know. Frankly, he probably wouldn't let her out of the kitchen until she told him what he wanted to know. He would probably strap her to the chair, shine a torch on her face and keep asking his wretched questions until she answered him.

And maybe he had a point. Roberto *was* very, very wealthy and could potentially be a target for gold-diggers. And she *was*, after all, seriously young to be his friend, even if she was only *passably attractive*. It was one thing to have no illusions about the way you looked. It was another thing to have someone point out your physical shortcomings without even bothering to be nice about it.

She *knew* that she wasn't blessed with knock-'em-dead looks. She had lived in London long enough to realise that the tall and skinny ruled the roost when it came to what was deemed sexy and attractive.

But had there been any need for him to point it out? The throwaway insult hovered at the back of her mind like a thorn. Odious man.

'Years…' Alessandro said, frowning. She wasn't lying.

Her face couldn't have been more transparent, and yet how was it that he hadn't even known of her existence?

'Before I went to London,' Laura confirmed. 'He belonged to the same gardening group as me and…as me. He loves horticulture, you know. And playing chess. Ever since I returned from London I've been playing chess with him once a week. He's a brilliant chess player.'

'You're telling me that the only interest you have in my father is as fellow chess player and gardener.'

'It's not solely about the gardening.' Laura bristled. 'It's the thrill of spotting rare plants, trying to produce interesting hybrids…' She noted the blank expression on his face. 'I don't suppose you have any plants where you live,' she tacked on. 'Roberto says that you live in a flat.'

'Penthouse apartment, and, no, no plants that I can think of offhand,' Alessandro responded automatically. 'So you play chess and talk about plants.'

'Pretty much.' The silence stretched between them until she began to fidget uncomfortably. 'It's called having hobbies. You must have some of those…'

'I work,' Alessandro replied shortly. 'And…' he suddenly smiled and just like that his face was transformed, the harsh, unyielding lines smoothed out to give a picture of mind-blowing sexiness '…I play. I consider both to be my hobbies…'

Colour had invaded her cheeks. Her green eyes were locked to his face. When she nervously licked her lips, she saw the way his eyes absently followed the movement and that made her go even redder. 'Play?' she asked feebly. Her brain seemed to have gone AWOL. He was still half smiling, his head inclined slightly to one side, and she was still beetroot red, uncomfortable in her own skin and not liking the sensation.

'Oh, yes,' he said smoothly. 'I'm very good at playing.'

Laura blinked and came back down to earth. 'Well, your father enjoys his chess and his plants and...'

'And?'

'This and that. He's had to take it easy after the stroke and, of course, he's only really now back on his feet properly after the fall, but he'll be back in the swing of things in no time at all.'

'What's *this and that*?' Trampolining? Abseiling? Whitewater rafting? He'd had no idea that his father was an active member of the local horticultural society so the *this and that* could literally, in his books, have applied to anything at all.

Laura shrugged evasively. 'Usual. The point is that he can start back doing all the stuff he enjoys now. So you can go back down to London, safe in the knowledge that he's well looked after. No need to feel duty bound to rush up here and check him over. Not to mention check over his friends and the people who work for him. No need for you to think that you have to keep an eye and give people the sack or dock their pay or whatever else you think might be necessary...'

Alessandro looked in wonderment at the pink-faced woman glaring defiantly at him. When was the last time he had encountered someone with such barefaced cheek? Actually, had he *ever*? Whatever angle women took with him, it never included being lippy.

'Before we get on to the juicy bit of what I have to say...' Alessandro relaxed back and crossed his legs, ankle resting lightly on his knee, hands linked on his lap. 'I'm curious.'

'What about?' Laura didn't care for his loose-limbed, relaxed pose because it resembled the looseness of a predator just before it homed in for a kill.

'About what brought you back from London to this...'

he looked around him, as though in search of an inspiring adjective '...backwater.'

Laura bristled. He was doing it again. Turning her into a self-defensive, shrieking harridan, which was not her at all.

She breathed in deeply and tried to think Zen thoughts. 'This isn't a *backwater*.' Her voice was quiet and even, even if her blood was boiling. 'If you took the time to really look around you, you'd see that it's one of the most beautiful places in the world. There's everything you could possibly hope to want in Scotland. There are castles, lochs, rivers and lakes, mountains... It's a wonderfully peaceful place...'

'Interesting travelogue. I'm more of an urban guy myself but is that an invitation to show me the sights and win me over?'

'It most certainly is not!'

Alessandro laughed, really laughed, with humour, his dark eyes lazy and amused as they rested on her flushed face.

'Shame,' he mused pensively. 'A personal tour might really go the distance in winning me over to its charms. So you moved here because there are castles and lakes and it's peaceful.'

Laura didn't actually think that her reasons for moving back to Scotland were any of the man's business but would he keep pressing? Secrets always engendered curiosity in other people and naturally she didn't care one way or another whether he was curious or not but still...why make things harder for herself?

'Partly, and also because my grandmother had a turn...' Which was somewhat true and left out the bigger part of her reason, namely her ill-advised, foolish love affair.

'Had a turn?'

'Was getting dizzy spells, suffering with her balance. She lives on her own and I wanted to be here for her.' She looked wistfully off into the distance. 'She was there for me when my parents died. I didn't begrudge returning to be here for her.'

Alessandro swiftly dispelled the glaring contradictions between them. He was here on behalf of his father, to take him down to London even though he might protest the move. It was for his own good! For a start, there was just so much choice when it came to various medical treatments, and having had both a stroke and a fall, who knew what medical treatment the future held for him? In London, he would receive the best!

'Big of you,' Alessandro murmured. 'I can only think that it must have been a wrench leaving the bright city lights and returning to all this peace and tranquillity. What was your job in London?'

He wasn't interested. Not really. He was simply establishing her credentials, working out whether she was a threat to his father's fortune or not. She knew that.

She wondered what had possessed her to come cycling here today and, having seen that SUV skewed in the courtyard, what had further possessed her to ring the doorbell, knowing that Roberto's son would be on the premises.

Fate had really decided to have a laugh at her expense.

'I worked as a PA.' She lowered her eyes, a little flicker of movement that Alessandro's keen antennae picked up.

'What company?'

'I don't know what that has to do with anything!' she snapped, bright spots of colour on her cheeks.

'You're right. It hasn't. And I wouldn't have asked if I'd known that I was getting too close to state secrets.'

'It's no big deal.' And yet, for some reason, she was reluctant to say the name of the firm out loud. Was it because she would be reminded of Colin? And the mortification of finding out that he had been lying to her? The horror of realising just how naive she had been to have handed over her trust to a smooth-talker? The shame when she thought that he had seen how green round the gills she'd been and had known that she would have lacked the experience to figure out what a bastard he really was?

She surfaced to find Alessandro's dark eyes pinned thoughtfully to her face and she tilted her chin stubbornly and told him the name of the company.

'Not,' she repeated, 'that it's any of your business.'

'I know the company,' he murmured, still looking at her in a way that made her feel as though he could see right down deep into the very core of her. 'And naturally I'm interested in finding out about one of my father's friends... Why wouldn't I be?'

'I didn't think you were ever interested before,' Laura pointed out. 'I mean, you could have come to visit when there have been things going on...joined in...'

'Things? What sort of things?'

'Oh, you know...we yokels try to have a barn dance at least once a month and let's not forget the annual hog roast while we all stand outside and admire the peaceful countryside...'

He burst out laughing. Suddenly those thoughtful eyes were dark with lazy appreciation.

Sexy, sharp-tongued, lippy...funny.

'I prefer the barn dances in London,' he told her with mock seriousness. 'And the hog roasts are good, too, although, of course, we all tend to stand outside and admire the pollution. Happy times...'

Laura didn't want to laugh but she had to fight the urge. 'It's good of you to visit him,' she admitted grudgingly.

'I suppose you've been worried but, like I said, there's no need. I try to check on him every day after work.'

'Oh? You managed to find yourself another PA job here?' He wasn't even sure what companies existed in the small town. He definitely wouldn't have put it down as somewhere with a flourishing employment sector.

'I realised that working as someone's personal assistant wasn't what I wanted to do.'

'No?'

'When I came back here, I landed a teaching job and it's very fulfilling. I teach at the local primary school. It's small and there are only a handful of kids in each class, but it's extremely rewarding.'

'Teacher.'

'The hours are convenient and, of course, there are the holidays and half-terms, and because it's a small village school I know all the mums on a one-to-one basis.' It was a terrific job, nothing to be ashamed of, and yet Laura couldn't stop the feeling of being just a little drab, just a tiny bit of a country bumpkin.

'Cosy.'

'I expect you must find it all very boring, but not everyone is consumed with wanting to live in a city and make pots of money.'

'I can't recall saying anything about finding what you do boring, although I question how much personal satisfaction you must get in a place as small as this, especially after living in London.'

'I got sick of the rat race,' she told him shortly, and his eyebrows shot up.

'Bit young to be jaded about that, wouldn't you say? Normally that's something that tends to afflict the over-forties. What about all the excitement?'

'I'd had it with excitement.'

'Ah,' Alessandro murmured, and she shot him a sharp, narrowed look, which he returned with bland innocence.

'Is that all? Have you finished questioning me? Maybe you could point me in the direction of your father, if, of course, I've passed the test.'

'He's in his greenhouse.' Alessandro jerked his head in the general direction of the back gardens but his eyes remained pinned to her face.

So she'd returned to her grandmother to lick her wounds. Maybe her grandmother really had had some kind of turn but he was sharp enough to get the lie of the land…she'd had some sort of unpleasant experience in London involving a guy, probably someone she worked with, judging from the shifty way she had talked about her place of work. She might wax lyrical about the peace and tranquillity and lakes and rivers, but the truth was that she'd had her heart broken and had returned to her comfort zone to patch herself up.

He found himself wondering what sort of guy she had got involved with and promptly nipped his curiosity in the bud because after this weekend he doubted he would ever lay eyes on the woman again.

Which was something of a shame. In fact, something of a shame he hadn't laid eyes on her before, on one of his rare forays into the Scottish wilds. She would certainly have made his duty visits a lot more alluring. Biting winds, depressingly bleak and empty countryside and his father's challenged conversational skills would definitely have been easier to endure…

'Right.' Laura stood up and thought that she should be feeling more relieved to be out of the presence of this odious man than she actually was.

'I wouldn't bother having the food conversation, though.'

'What are you talking about?'

'You mentioned that you had cycled over to do your Good Samaritan duty...an offer to go food shopping for him, as if my father doesn't have the wherewithal to pay someone to do that on his behalf. Actually—and I'm sure you know this—he could pay a chef to buy the food and cook it if he wanted. It would certainly spare him the stuff Freya churns out...'

Laura did her best not to agree with him. She had a good enough relationship with Freya, who occasionally cracked a half-smile in her presence, but no one could say that the woman produced haute cuisine.

'Your father likes plain, simple food.'

'Just as well. With sour-faced Freya at the helm, it's all he's ever likely to get.'

'Why shouldn't I ask him if he needs anything?'

'Because there's no point filling the cupboards only to empty them again in the space of a few days. Waste of time.'

'What? What are you talking about?' Laura stared at that drop-dead-gorgeous, arrogant face and subsided back into her chair like a puppet whose strings had suddenly been cut.

'There's a reason I've come up here,' Alessandro explained calmly. 'I've spoken to my father about this on a number of occasions, and I've emailed him...' He sighed heavily and flung his head back, half closing his eyes as he thought about the frustration of dealing with someone who didn't want to face the inevitable. It shouldn't be like this. He knew that. Of course, history couldn't be altered any more than the present could be changed...but it shouldn't be like this, a constant uphill struggle.

'I'm confused,' Laura said urgently. 'Spoken to him about what? Emailed him about what?'

Alessandro opened his eyes and looked at her in silence

for a few seconds. 'He hasn't confided in you, then. Odd, considering you're supposed to be best buddies.'

'Please stop being sarcastic and tell me what's going on.'

'I've come up here to take my father back down to London with me.'

'Take him?' Laura looked at him in complete bewilderment. 'Take him down for a few days?'

'Not quite,' he said gently. 'Brace yourself. Roberto's stint here in Scotland is at an end. I'm taking him down to London with me and he won't be returning. The house will be packed up, necessities shipped down to London, the rest removed for auction. I've bought him an apartment in Chelsea. It's the right size and if he's in London I can keep an eye on him.'

Laura was finding it hard to keep track of what he was saying because none of it made any sense.

'You're kidding. Aren't you?'

'I never kid about things like that. Hasn't he mentioned any of this to you? On any of your Little Red Riding Hood visits?'

For a second, Laura wanted to throw something at him. How could he just sit here, discussing the future of an old man, talking about it in a voice that was dry and cool and caustic?

'You,' she hissed in a driven undertone, 'are the most... the most...'

'Spit it out. I assure you I won't take it personally.'

'The most *obnoxious* person I have *ever* met in my entire life! It's no wonder that...'

'That *what*?'

They stared at each other in silence. Laura could hear the pounding of her heart, could feel the blood rushing hotly through her veins. 'That nothing...' she muttered, casting her eyes downwards. She had raced towards a cliff and almost flung herself over the side. What did she know of the relationship between father and son? She surmised. Roberto had never come out and said anything derogatory about Alessandro, but the cold distance between them was as obvious as a neon sign in a dark street.

The truth was that it was not really her business. And because the man sitting opposite her rattled her, it did not give her the excuse to say things that shouldn't be said or to voice thoughts that should remain in her head.

Alessandro chose to let that go.

Did he really want to find out what might have been said about him behind his back? No! This was how it was between his father and himself but he wasn't going to put himself through unnecessary irritation by having an outside party share their opinion on the situation. No way.

He looked at her coldly, noting her discomfort and choosing not to relieve her of it.

'He hasn't breathed a word of this to me or to... Well, I'm shocked. Beyond shocked. I can't believe you're going to try to wrench poor Roberto away from everything he... he holds dear and fling him into the mad chaos of London life. You can't. You just can't!'

'No need to panic,' Alessandro murmured in a soft voice that sent chills racing through her. 'It's a spacious three-bedroom apartment. All mod cons, including en suite bathrooms. I'm sure he'll keep a bedroom free for his special friends.' He was repulsed by the thought of her having anything to do with his father beyond the purely platonic. Yes, she had denied that connection, but if that were the case, why the horror and dismay?

Why the extreme reaction? She looked as distraught as Chicken Little when the sky was falling down.

His lips thinned and she knew exactly what he was

getting at. Where was a heavy object when you needed one? she fumed.

'And if he hasn't mentioned anything to you,' Alessandro inserted smoothly, 'I put that down to denial. Because I've been having this conversation with my father for the past six months.'

Laura looked at him in stunned silence.

'He's old...'

'My point exactly! The stroke...the fractured pelvis... He can't deal with this bloody great big mansion. He needs somewhere more compact. He needs to be able to make it to his bedroom from the kitchen in under three hours.'

'Please don't exaggerate. Like you said, Roberto could afford as much help as he wants to. At the moment he just has Freya and Fergus, but I'm sure he would employ someone else to help him if he thought he needed it.'

'This isn't a subject that's open to debate. I'm not thrusting him into a rabbit hutch in the centre of the city. He'll adjust. London is full of exciting things.'

'Old people don't want excitement,' Laura said flatly. 'They want routine. They want stability. They want to be surrounded by the people and faces they're familiar with.'

Alessandro stared at her with incredulity. Were they talking about the same man?

'And how often are you going to visit him?' she pursued, ignoring his closed expression. 'Are you going to make sure he settles in? Will you be taking him under your wing? Or will you be visiting him four times a year but happily with a much shorter journey?'

Alessandro scowled. 'Your concern is touching but I assure you...he'll be just fine. And, incidentally, who are these familiar faces he needs to surround himself with?'

'He has lots of friends in the village.'

'Aside from you?'

'Yes, aside from me! What do you think he does during the days? I mean, I know his health hasn't been great recently, but before that? And now that he's on the mend?'

Alessandro looked at her blankly.

'You don't know, do you? You haven't got a clue. You want to drag him away from his home and you can't even be bothered to find out what he'll be missing! What his life here is all about!'

'You're shouting.'

'I *never* shout!' Her voice reverberated in the silence and she glared at him. 'I *usually* never shout,' she amended, 'but I'm just so…angry. And stop staring at me. I suppose you've never been shouted at by anyone in your life before?'

'Correct.'

Drawn out of her state of shock, Laura peered suspiciously at him. 'No one ever gets mad at you?' she asked incredulously. 'Ever?'

'You're looking at me as though you find that hard to believe,' Alessandro returned coolly. Taking away the physical side of things, on every level this woman offended him on all fronts. He had no thoughts one way or another on other people and the choices they made in terms of relationships. As far as he was concerned, the rest of humanity could hurl themselves into pointless marriages like lemmings jumping off a cliff, only to find themselves picking up the pieces and counting the pennies when those marriages crashed and burned. Which most of them did.

As for himself, he had no intention, and never had, of getting wrapped up with any woman. He had led a life that was ruled by his head and he liked that. Maybe the cold withdrawal of his only parent had pointed him down that path. It wasn't something he had wasted his time analysing. He just knew that, for him, women were there to be savoured and enjoyed until the time came for him to push on. They were his stress-free zone, a welcome break from the enjoyable frenzy of being at the top of the game in the world of business.

A woman who shouted did not constitute a stress-free zone.

'I do,' Laura said truthfully.

'Women, especially, fall into that category.'

'I find that even harder to believe.'

'I don't encourage temper tantrums,' he said smoothly. 'There's something about a screaming woman I don't find a turn-on.'

Just as well my aim isn't to turn you on, Laura thought. The pulse in her throat kicked up a steady beat. She took in his lazy sprawl, the brooding night-dark gaze of his eyes, the harsh, perfect contours of his face, and something inside her flared into unwelcome, unexpected life.

Suddenly confused, she banked it down.

'I just think that before you start trying to pull the rug from underneath someone's feet, you should make an effort to understand where they're coming from and what they would lose. Doesn't your father have any say in this? Or are you going to stampede through his objections and do what *you* think is best?'

'This conversation is going round in circles.' Alessandro raked his fingers impatiently through his hair, spared her a searing glance and then stood up to help himself to a bottle of water from the fridge, which he drank in one long swallow. Then he leaned against the kitchen counter and looked at her. 'I'll do what I consider best for my father and you can pull all the hysterical, emotive language out of the bag, but nothing is going to change that. Like I told

you, I've talked to my father about this. If he chose not to
keep you in the loop, then what can I say?' He shrugged
and stared at her flushed face.

'There's something you should know,' Laura said grudgingly, and Alessandro stilled.

'I'm all ears.'

'It's not just that your father has a social life in the village, and if...' she looked at him with a flare of unchar-
acteristic rebellion in her wide, green eyes '...he chose to
keep you out of the loop, then what can I say? He's also...
well...you probably have cut-and-dried opinions on love,
but he's involved with someone locally...'

For a few seconds, and for maybe the first time in his
life, Alessandro was rendered speechless. Her words fil-
tered into his consciousness, tried to take shape but then
dissolved before they could link up and make any sense.

'Did you just hear what I said?'

'I heard you. I'm just not following... You're telling me
that my father *has a girlfriend*?'

'My gran.'

Perplexed, Alessandro shook his head in an attempt to
get the connections in his brain to start working.

Laura saw his bewilderment and suddenly, out of nowhere, she felt a sharp pang of sympathy and compas-
sion for him. Didn't this say everything there was to say
about the kind of relationship he had with Roberto? One
in which nothing personal was ever discussed? In which
no emotion was ever allowed to surface? How on earth
had that happened?

'My father is going out with your...your grandmother?
How does that even make sense?'

'It's easy,' Laura said drily. 'They met ages ago and have
been friends for a long time, but in the past few months,

a bit longer, actually, they've begun seeing one another.
Going on dates, that kind of thing…'

'My father *goes on dates*?'

'It happens. Two people have a solid friendship…one
thing leads to another… He's still an attractive guy. I'd
bet there are a few ladies in the gardening club who have
had their eye on him.'

Alessandro walked back to the table, sat down, stared
off for a few frowning moments into space, then focused
on the woman looking at him, head inclined, her soft lips
parted.

'Details.'

'I beg your pardon?'

'How long exactly has this dating game been going on?
And your grandmother…where does she live? Widowed?
Divorced? How old is she?'

Laura tensed, predicting the direction of his assump-
tions. 'You've accused me of being a gold-digger,' she said
coldly. 'You couldn't have been further from the truth. And
don't you even dare think of implying that my grandmother
is after your dad's money, either! They're just two people
who get along and enjoy one another's company. If you
want the bare details, here they are.

'My grandmother lives in a little house on the outskirts
of the village about twenty minutes away. She's lived here
all her life and, yes, she's widowed. My grandfather passed
on more years ago than I care to think. She never really
thought about ever finding anyone else, least of all someone she's known since for ever, but, then, it's really only
in the past ten years or so that your father has really begun
integrating himself into the community. He was quite re-
clusive before that. I guess work kept him away a lot…and
of course my gran would have been busy working in the
neighbouring town. She ran the garden centre there. Only

gave up five years ago because the travel was getting a bit of a nuisance, especially in the winter. 'Course, she drove there, but you have no idea how freez—'

'I'm getting the picture. Age?'

'Huh? Oh. Right. Seventy-six. So that's just one of the reasons why it would be heartbreaking for you to charge up here and try to force him to leave.'

'Charge? Force? Heartbreaking?'

But this put a new spin on things. Maybe he should personally check out the situation. His father was dating someone whose granddaughter was his best buddy. Cynicism was ingrained in Alessandro, as much a vital part of him as drawing breath. Could this pair be working in tandem? It was far-fetched but sometimes far-fetched turned out to be reality and it always paid to be on the safe side, especially when tens of millions of pounds were at stake.

'You're right.'

'I am?' Laura looked at him warily, trying to see behind that thoughtful, speculative expression.

'If my father is to leave this place, then it's not up to me to be heavy-handed. I need to persuade him that there's life beyond the Scottish boundaries...'

'He won't be persuaded, I'm sure of that.'

Alessandro dealt her a slashing smile. So this weekend might not happen, but that was fine. He was the kind of guy who could think outside the box when it came to dealing with unexpected situations. Like this. And, being perfectly honest, the lush appeal of the woman currently looking at him as though she expected him to produce a bomb from up his sleeve would certainly introduce a bit of entertainment to the menu.

'But worth a try, wouldn't you agree? I mean, you've spent the past hour wringing your hands and wailing that

I'm being unfair. So I'm sure you'd have no objections to…
showing me first-hand this fuzzy, warm social life my father would be so loath to leave behind…'

CHAPTER THREE

'BOY'S LATE. PROBABLY changed his mind. Probably decided that it'd be better to airlift me out of my own damned house than go through this charade of pretending he's interested in anything I do!'

Laura looked at Roberto anxiously. Alessandro was half an hour late and who better than she to know the vagaries of transport? Trains that laughed in the face of timetables. Cabs that got stuck in traffic and crawled along as though they were submerged in treacle. Planes that hovered and circled and hovered and circled because they were at the back of a queue.

'He said he'd come,' she told him firmly while sneaking a glance at her watch. It was nearly six and the two of them were hovering like maiden aunts waiting for their wayward charge to return home.

It was ridiculous.

'My son has his own damned personal schedule! Lives for his work!' He repositioned his tie and banged his walking stick on the wooden floor. 'Probably got a call and, of course, any call would take precedence over coming to Scotland! Never *could* stand the place! Always preferred that namby-pamby London life!' He threw her a sly look. ''Course, something else could have held him up!'

'Yes?' She looked at Roberto affectionately. He still belonged to an era when ties were de rigueur, whatever the occasion, and trousers were always belted firmly at the waist. He was dressed in a jumper with the crisp white shirt underneath neatly buttoned to the neck, the knot of his dark, striped tie crisply in place and a pair of his most casual slacks, which were still pressed into submission with no-nonsense creases down the middle of the legs. His shoes gleamed. He looked such a vision that she had taken a picture of him on her phone so that she could send it to her grandmother. He had, naturally, grumbled, although she'd noticed that he had surreptitiously neatened his thick silver hair with his hand before the shot.

'Floozy.'

'Sorry?'

'Floozy. Has enough of them chasing behind him! Met one or two myself. Silly little airheads but sometimes even the smartest of men can't resist a—'

'I get the picture, Roberto!' She led him away from that subject back to plants and gardens and the cookery club her grandmother wanted him to join.

The last thing she needed was to hear about Alessandro and his so-called floozies.

In fact, the last thing she wanted was to be here, on a Friday evening, wearing a long-sleeved, knee-length dress and boots and waiting for a guy who had managed to get under her skin in a very, very irritating way. She had spent the past week thinking about him, hadn't been able to shake him out of her head, and having to face him again was not what she wanted.

But here she was because Roberto had told her that the three of them would be going out.

'Got it into his head that the old man's life's suddenly interesting!' Roberto had announced. 'Told him it was a damned sight more interesting than one that was just work, work, work and some floozies in between!' After that he had sat her down and explained the whole business of the move he didn't want and wasn't going to be forced into. He hadn't been able to bring himself to discuss it with her grandmother and she wasn't to say a word. He would talk to Edith himself when she returned, not, he insisted, that he was going anywhere.

'But if the boy wants to try to move me, then he can try all he wants! He'll soon find out that this old bugger won't be going anywhere!'

Laura had picked up the thread of trepidation running through his bravado and had instantly agreed to be by his side when Alessandro arrived. She would not, emphatically *would not*, be sticking around for the entire weekend but, yes, she would accompany them to dinner at the newly opened fish restaurant in the neighbouring town.

Now Roberto was fretting but before she could start soothing him all over again they heard an overhead roar and they both hurried over to the big bay window, peered out and registered the presence of a helicopter, which was circling, finding the right spot in the immense garden outside, before landing. The blindingly bright beam cutting through the darkness was an impressive sight. Laura would put money on every single person in the town craning their necks out of their windows and wondering what the heck was going on.

'Might have guessed he wouldn't have come like any other person!' He was already hobbling out of the sitting room, where they had been chatting in front of a pot of tea, and Laura sprinted after him, reaching the front door just as it was opened and there he was, as tall, as sinfully good-looking, as aristocratically arrogant as she remembered.

'Hope you haven't set that thing down on any of my plants!' Roberto bellowed as the rotors wound down to a noisy din.

Alessandro glanced wryly past him to catch Laura's eye and her skin was suddenly on fire.

'And thank you for that warm welcome.' Alessandro turned back to signal something to his pilot, then stepped into the hall, shutting the door behind him. His sharp eyes didn't miss a thing. His father still had the same mutinous expression on his face as he had had the weekend before, when Alessandro had tried to get him to talk about moving, and Laura...

She'd been on his mind. He hadn't been able to work that one out. Was it because, in a sea of predictable women, she had been the only one to have ever contradicted him? Had the novelty of being criticised got under his skin and provoked a reaction? Like nettle rash? Something annoying you couldn't ignore? Or had the lack of a female presence in his life had something to do with it? It had been a couple of months since he had seen off his last girlfriend.

He didn't analyse the reaction. He just knew that the weekend planned had lain in front of him, glittering like a gem on the horizon. And that, in itself, was spectacular, considering how reluctant his visits had been in the past, obligatory visits to be endured before returning to the sanity of city life.

'You're late. Was about to head to the kitchen and take something out of the fridge!'

He glanced at Laura to see whether she, like him, was irritated with his father's impatience, but when he looked at her it was to see that she was smiling indulgently at Roberto, her hand resting lightly on his forearm, a gesture of affection that his father appeared to take for granted.

'If Freya stocks the fridge,' Alessandro said evenly, 'then I wouldn't count on the contents to be inspiring. I'll be ten minutes at the most. I need to send a quick email.'

Laura frowned. She knew that Roberto had been

dressed and waiting for the past hour and a half. She'd helped him with his tie and she'd seen, from the other three ties draped over the back of the chair, that he'd had a task choosing the one he wanted to wear.

'I think we should head off sooner rather than later,' she murmured, catching Alessandro's eye and holding it. 'Roberto always has an early night.'

'Roberto can go to bed whenever he damned well wants to!' Roberto announced, but she felt him relax a little when Alessandro immediately nodded and dumped his case on the floor.

'I'm having a car delivered to me in the morning.' Alessandro fished his mobile out of his pocket. 'What's the number for the local taxi company?'

'No need,' Laura said briskly. She hooked her arm through Roberto's and then turned to him and tucked his scarf neatly into his overcoat.

'You're always faffing and fussing, girl!'

But again Alessandro was made aware of a relationship he had never even known existed, a relationship from which he was made to feel like an outsider. His father, grumbling and chiding, was clearly pleased to have her fuss over him.

'Someone has to when my grandmother isn't around,' she murmured, and Roberto shot his son a sidelong look before shooing her away. 'There's no need to call a taxi.' She stood back, head cocked, making sure everything was up to her inspection with Roberto's outfit. 'I've brought my car.'

'You're going to drive us?' Alessandro let them pass and slammed the door behind them.

'Don't tell me you don't feel comfortable with a woman behind the wheel,' she said with saccharine sweetness. 'Because if that's the case, then you're a dinosaur.'

'Girl speaks her mind!' Roberto chortled smugly. 'Something you'll have to get used to, my boy!' He absently patted her hand as they trundled towards the side of the house.

'You intend to take us out in *that*?' Squatting directly under one of the security lights that surrounded the house was an ageing Morris Minor. 'I thought those cars were extinct,' he murmured. 'Along with the dinosaurs you mentioned.'

'It's very reliable,' Laura told him tartly.

'Except for last winter,' Roberto pointed out, and for the duration of the drive they launched into an extended anecdote about the unpredictability of her car, which, Alessandro assumed, he was supposed to find uproariously hilarious. He wondered why his father didn't just buy her something more reliable and then grimaced because had he done that, Alessandro knew that *he* would have been the first to point out that his father was being ripped off.

He had intended to bring up the matter of the move but, over a surprisingly good meal, he found every effort thwarted.

They had in-jokes. They talked about people in the village. They spent way too long discussing some orchids someone or other had done something or other with, only desisting when Alessandro was forced to butt in and shut down that particular topic or risk falling asleep. He heard his father laugh. Twice. The sound was so unusual that he wondered whether his ears had been playing up but, no, at the end of an hour and a half he could see for himself that the life he had envisioned his father having might have been slightly off target.

And he had known nothing about it.

'So how long will you be staying?' Laura asked politely,

when, engine still running, they were back at the manor house.

'This has been the most uncomfortable journey of my life,' Alessandro informed her as he levered his big body out of the back seat. 'Why is your engine still running? I take it you're coming in.'

'I hadn't intended to.'

'Girl's got to be on her way!' Roberto announced.

'In that case,' Alessandro countered, 'we can have some time to discuss your move.'

'Not tonight, my boy. This old man needs his beauty sleep!'

'I'll come in for a couple of minutes.'

Roberto, on his way to the front door, paused to look at the two of them, eyes narrowed. 'Can't think Edith will want you gallivanting all over the country at this time of the night!'

Laura laughed as she joined them to walk to the front door. Roberto's bushy brows were drawn together in a frown. 'Hardly *gallivanting* all over the country,' she soothed. 'My grandmother worries too much.'

'With good cause,' Roberto muttered, rapping his walking stick on the front door impatiently as Alessandro jangled a bunch of keys, hunting out the right one. 'After all those shenanigans in London!'

'Here we go!' Laura trilled, hoping to drown out that utterly, utterly inappropriate remark and mentally vowing to warn her grandmother about any more confidences while Alessandro was on the scene, earwigging. 'Back home and I must say the meal was delicious!'

Much as she didn't want to spend time in Alessandro's company, she knew that she would have to, at least for half an hour or so. First, she wanted to find out how long he intended staying in Scotland, because having a car delivered was not a good sign. Second, she was desperate to know whether he was rethinking his silly decision to try to browbeat Roberto into moving down to London.

She had seen the way Roberto had deflected all attempts to manoeuvre the conversation to the move and she knew that whatever relationship the two had, it would crash and burn completely if Alessandro kept hammering away at his father, trying to force a move that wasn't wanted.

Couldn't he see that?

Did he care?

And how on earth had these two ended up at such loggerheads...?

She was curious. She shouldn't be but she was. She was waved aside when she offered to walk Roberto up the stairs and it was only when he had disappeared from sight that she felt the power of Alessandro's presence wrap around her like a stranglehold.

In the busyness of leaving the house and driving to the restaurant and then doing her utmost to carry the conversation to any topic that would demonstrate Roberto's ties to the community, she had forgotten how uncomfortable she felt in the dress.

Now, as those dark eyes settled on her, she had to stop herself from tugging it down.

'Drink?' He looked at her for a few seconds. She was wearing a dress that was never going to win prizes at a fashion show. It was an awkward length and, twinned with serviceable boots, gave the impression of someone who wasn't into clothes. His was a rich diet of catwalk models but he had still found his eyes straying time and time again over dinner to the way the fabric stretched over her full breasts, the way the neckline offered just a glimpse of cleavage, enough for his imagination to take flight. 'Because I'm guessing that the only reason you volunteered to come in was because there's something you want to say to me. A stiff gin and tonic might move things along.'

Laura scowled. With no Roberto around, he was back to being the arrogant, obnoxious guy who thought it was amusing to needle her. She could also tell from the way his eyes had skimmed over her that he found her get-up funny—the dress, which hadn't seen the light of day since London, and even then had only been worn once, the boots, which were sturdy, useful and most of all warm, but hardly the height of fashion.

He headed towards the kitchen and she traipsed along behind him. In a dark jumper and dark trousers, he was just impossibly sexy and she really resented the way she even *noticed* that when she didn't want to. She halted at the door and watched as he sauntered towards a cupboard, fetched two squat glasses and poured them both a drink.

'So,' he drawled, handing her a glass, 'are you going to remain standing by the door like a sentry or are you going to sit down and say what you have to say?'

His fingers had brushed against hers and every muscle and nerve in her body had reacted.

'You never mentioned how long you intended staying here…' She inched her way towards the table and sat down. The first sip of the gin and tonic was pretty frightful but the second sip was much better and helped her relax.

'Undecided. Why? Do I make you feel uncomfortable? I wouldn't want to put a spoke in the wheel, but…' he shrugged, sipped his drink and looked at her over the rim of his glass '…needs must.'

'What needs?'

'That's a somewhat leading question, wouldn't you say?' If they were referring to *his* needs, then he might very well meet them by staying.

He had a vivid image of her in his bed, sprawled in all

her glorious, lush beauty, her delicate, heart-shaped face heated with desire, her body his for the taking. He imagined her huge, green eyes riveted to his nakedness, her arms spread wide, her legs likewise…

Blood surged through him and he felt a fast, hard, painful erection.

'You were desperate for me to discover the ins and outs of my father's busy life here and if I'm to do that I'm going to have to rely on more than a question-and-answer session.' His voice was terse as he dispelled the sudden eroticism of his thoughts. 'For starters, answering questions has never been my father's speciality. When it comes to answering *personal* questions…well, put it this way, I don't foresee him putting out the welcome mat. Father-and-son chats have just never gone down that road.'

'Why?'

'Come again?'

'You should be able to have an honest, heart-to-heart conversation with Roberto when it comes to something as important as this. He should tell you why he doesn't want to move to London.'

'And yet, as you've seen for yourself, that sort of explanation hasn't been forthcoming, which is why I've gone ahead and done what I've considered best all round.'

'So why are you bothering to stay here if you've already made your mind up?'

'Because I want to see first-hand what the situation is with my father and your grandmother,' he said bluntly.

'Meaning?'

'I want to make sure that it's all above board.'

'I can't believe you just said that!'

'Why?' He shrugged. 'We've been through this before. You might as well accept that I'm not one of these idealistic, trusting types who takes whatever's told to him as the whole truth and nothing but the truth.'

'You are just *so cynical*. Isn't it enough that your father has found someone at his age? Someone who makes his life a better place?'

'Beautiful. And even more beautiful if that someone has his physical well-being at heart and frankly couldn't care less about the well-being of his bank account.'

Laura ground her teeth and glared at him. How was it that someone so good-looking could be so…cold?

But, then, Colin had been good-looking as well, hadn't he? And he'd turned out to be as genuine as a three-pound note. She obviously had a problem when it came to her judgement. She obviously was one of those people who could be swayed by good looks. Well, it had happened once before and it wasn't going to happen again.

And there was a big difference between Colin and Alessandro. Colin had been suave and charming. Alessandro was just…outspoken, arrogant and downright *charmless*.

If he had any reserves of charm, he wasn't going to use up any of his supply on *her*, at any rate.

And when it came to attractiveness…the differences were extreme as well, once you started looking a little more closely. Colin had been attractive in a *sanitised* way. His blond hair had always looked ever so slightly *helped along with products*, his smile had dazzled, his body had been slim and trim but not overtly muscular.

Alessandro, on the other hand, was good-looking in a more raw, untamed way. Underneath the sophistication you could half sense something more elemental, something powerful that was barely leashed.

And thank the Lord for that, she thought. Because that made her far safer from his brand of good looks!

'Gran is away until next week.' She reined in the desire to get into a shouting fit with him.

'And I can't wait to meet her.'

'And once you've sized her up, what do you intend to do?'

'I enjoy crossing bridges when I get to them.' Not strictly speaking true. He was a guy who had always preferred to plan in advance. However, in this instance he would have to think out of the box and react accordingly. The disturbing truth was that he had planned on a more clear-cut situation and was realising that that was not the case. He had counted on his father's stubbornness. What he hadn't counted on was the fact that that stubbornness was not misplaced if he saw himself as being dragged away from connections he would find difficult to replace in London.

But the thorny issue of trekking back and forth remained. Maybe if he and his father had had anything remotely resembling a functioning relationship, that situation might have been different. Maybe then those journeys wouldn't have been seen as a nuisance. But why beat around the bush? They didn't and Alessandro wasn't thrilled at the thought of having to make more and more inconvenient trips, staying for longer and longer periods of time, should his father's health nosedive.

He might not be lining up to receive the son of the year award, but neither was he so lacking in a sense of filial duty that he would be able to switch off completely.

'Don't you have to be…er…back in London? Running your company?'

'Companies. Plural. I have more than one and, no, I can take some time out to assess this situation.' He sighed suddenly and raked his fingers through his hair. 'It's not ideal,' he admitted. 'I didn't think I'd end up having to spend time here, checking up on a life I had no idea my father had. It makes things…slightly more problematic.'

Laura swallowed the last of her drink. She'd had nothing to drink over dinner as she had been driving and now the gin and tonic rushed pleasantly to her head, warming her and making her feel relaxed, not as defensive. He looked weary. Still sexy as hell, but weary.

'I don't know why you have the relationship you have with Roberto,' she was startled to hear herself say, 'but if you try to force his hand, it'll backfire. You might end up dragging him down to London but it would be against his will and he'll resent you for it for the rest of his life.'

'I don't recall asking for your opinion.'

'Do you *ever* ask for anyone's opinion?'

'No.'

'Sometimes it pays to hear what other people have to say.' She felt some of her Dutch courage ooze away in the face of his icy stare. 'You can't be a rock all of the time…'

Except he was and always had been. He'd grown up knowing that he was on his own and he had acquired the necessary independence from an early age. She, it would appear, had not. Even though…

'How old were you when you lost your parents?' He gave in to the curiosity that had been nibbling at the edges of his consciousness. He didn't encourage deep and meaningful conversations with women because deep and meaningful unfailingly gave rise to awkward forward thinking on their part. There was nothing he disliked more than a woman with plans and too much interest from him engendered plans. But…this was different. Exceptional circumstances. Curiosity was permitted.

'Seven.' She was startled at his digression.

'And then you moved in with your grandmother.'

'She was my closest living relative and we'd always been close.'

'And despite the loss of your parents, you remain an optimistic, upbeat person. That...' he sat forward, scarcely believing that he was having this conversation '...is because your grandmother was a constant. I think you're viewing the relationship I have with my father through rose-tinted spectacles.

'He paid the exorbitant school fees for my boarding school, lavished as much pocket money on me as any boy could possibly want or need, paid for ridiculously expensive holidays, which I took with various trusted members of staff, and those were the constant. His presence wasn't because I seldom laid eyes on him and when I did, we were forced into agonisingly polite conversation that we were both very happy to bring to an end as soon as we could.' He couldn't believe he had said as much as he had. It was so unlike him to confide in anyone. It made him feel annoyed and uncomfortable at the same time but he told himself that it had been necessary, if only to combat her perky optimism. She was a one-woman cheerleading team.

'What about your mother?' Laura's heart went out to him. In fact, she wanted to close the distance between them and place her hand over his.

'What about her?' This was a subject that was closed to all. It was something he rarely thought about. He had put to bed all questions about his mother a long time ago. His mother had died when he had been young enough not to have remembered her...an unexpected heart complication that had sprung from nowhere. That was the sum total of what he knew.

'Your father has never mentioned her,' Laura said wistfully. 'I know he came here without a wife all those years ago. No one saw much of him at all. He was never around.

He lived in the big house and half the time no one knew whether he was in the house or not.'

'And no doubt everyone had a theory.'

'I don't know. I was busy at school, then I went away to university and then down to London. By then he had stopped working, I guess, and had begun to appear in the town with a little more regularity.'

'I'm struggling to picture my father strolling into the village on a Sunday morning for a cup of tea and chit-chat with the locals.'

'That might be because you don't really know him.'

Alessandro's lips thinned. 'And it's so important to really get to know people, isn't it?' he remarked with smooth assurance. He strolled to pour them both another drink and she half-heartedly swatted the offer away.

'I have to drive back.'

Alessandro didn't answer that. He perched on the table, which meant that she had to look up at him, and their eyes met. The slow flush that crawled into her cheeks was telling him something and he never, ever, got it wrong when it came to those little signals women emanated.

His dark eyes dropped to her mouth and he deliberately let them linger there, and the way she nervously licked her lips was also telling him something.

The fire that had been running through his veins like a deep, underground, fast-flowing river began surfacing.

He wasn't into self-denial when it came to sex. What was the point? If it was there, he took it. It was there now. Did she even know that? Was she even aware of the attraction she felt towards him or was she too busy trying to analyse him and probe beneath the surface?

'And, yes, it's important you really get to…er…you know, find out about Roberto before you do anything that could…um…really throw him into turmoil…' Laura's eyes skittered away from his, although her skin felt as hot as fire. She could still feel those deep, dark eyes of his locked onto her and it was rousing stuff in her that she didn't want.

Alessandro Falcone was off limits and it had a lot more to do with the complicated situation between them.

He was off limits because he was just plain wrong on every single level.

He was everything she didn't want in her life. When she'd walked away from London, from her job and from a guy who had strung her along with his charm and his dashing good looks, she had made a quiet resolution to herself that she would not get involved with anyone who wasn't open, sincere and basically just like her. Normality was what she wanted in a guy. Even if she were to have a fling, it would be with someone whose values she shared and who wasn't out to get what he could. It wouldn't be with one of life's takers.

So why was it that she felt naked and exposed when he looked at her like that?

'We could spend the rest of the night discussing my father,' Alessandro murmured. He moved, strolled to the window, which offered the view of a pitch-dark night outside, strolled back to the table and resumed his position, perching on it but this time closer to her. Close enough for her breathing to feel a little restricted.

'But let's talk about you instead. You've done a lot of low-level, amateur psychoanalysis on me... Fair's fair. What was my father referring to when he mentioned your shenanigans in London?'

'I don't know what you're talking about.'

'Please tell me that you're not one of those hypocrites who are forthright and direct when it comes to mouthing off their opinions on other people's lives but clam up the second someone tries to get a straight answer out of them about their own lives. That would be disappointing…'

Laura glared at him angrily. Hypocrite? That was one accusation that had never been levelled against her! Too outspoken, yes. Naive, yes. Too honest for her own good, definitely! But hypocritical? No.

'Lost for words?' Alessandro asked silkily. 'And yet you've been so vocal up until now…'

'You know what the older generation is like,' she hedged through gritted teeth. 'They gossip.'

'I never took my father for a gossiper,' Alessandro commented truthfully.

'Well, he is when he's with my grandmother. And you know…people of that generation think that walking in a park holding hands with someone if you're not engaged to be married comes under the heading of *shenanigans*!'

'Have you buried yourself here to escape a broken relationship?'

The mildness of his voice was disconcerting because his eyes were shrewd and perceptive.

'I don't consider this a graveyard.'

'So you had an ill-advised fling with someone you worked with. It fell apart at the seams. It happens.'

'Who told you that?' She looked at him narrowly. 'I suppose Roberto let slip.'

'Like I told you, my father and I are not on such familiar terms. I guessed and it seems that I was right.'

She looked away. Her hands were trembling and she linked her fingers together, stilling them. She didn't want to talk about this, wasn't going to talk about it, and yet wasn't he right when he'd said that she had felt free to probe but when the shoe was on the other foot, she wasn't quite so ready to confide?

Was this her Achilles' heel? The place where her insecurities lay? Being brought up by her grandmother had been good, better than good, but she had never really caught on to make-up and feminine wiles—not in the way her other classmates had. Her grandmother had simply been beyond all that by the time Laura had hit her teens. When it came to the art of flirting, she was at a loss and so Colin and the way he had used her inexperience had hit her hard, had reinforced all those insecurities.

She couldn't shake it off because she didn't know how. She wasn't casual enough when it came to men. Would she *ever* be able to shake it off? Alessandro was right, wasn't he? She'd buried herself here and she wondered, in a sudden surge of panic, whether she would remain buried. Would she ever venture out into the big, bad world again? Dip her feet back into the water?

Or would that prospect seem scarier and scarier the more time passed by? The only interaction with guys she had here was with the partners of the friends she had grown up with, who had left and returned or else had never left. She would end up batty and alone and talking to herself at inappropriate times in public places.

'You're not going to cry on me, are you?'

'No, I'm not!' Laura snapped fiercely. 'And, *yes*, I did have a situation with someone I worked with. Satisfied? He strung me along and then I found out that he was married!'

'He was just another bastard.'

'You don't understand! I really trusted Colin Scott. I thought he was a decent kind of guy but it turned out that he was a liar without any morals. So, yes, I came back here. Go on, say it… I'm a loser and an idiot.'

'Is that what you think?'

'What else?' she asked bitterly.

'You were blindsided by a creep but you don't have to bury yourself and lick your wounds.'

'No? What would you suggest?' she muttered. 'I'm not licking my wounds. I'm just…taking time out…'

'Well, there *is* one thing I would suggest.'

'What's that? I'm all ears, as you would say.'

'Step back into those muddy waters.' He stood up and flexed his muscles. It had been a while since he had done any chasing. He wondered whether he was rusty but, no, she was looking up at him with dawning comprehension. He wondered whether it was a good idea to go there but, then, they were both adults, weren't they? And once the ground rules were laid…

'Only next time round,' he said softly, 'make sure you know exactly what you're dealing with. I find that works for me. I'm honest upfront. Sex with no strings attached. No future plans made. No promises to be broken.' He smiled crookedly and stroked a stray tendril of hair away from her face, felt her breathing quicken, saw the way her pupils dilated.

'From where I'm standing, that's the way forward. The waters might still be a little muddy but they'd be a hell of a lot safer than quicksand…'

CHAPTER FOUR

HEART BEATING so hard she felt as though she might pass out, Laura inched back in the chair but she couldn't peel her eyes away from his face.

'I should be leaving,' she managed to croak. 'I don't... don't want to be driving late at night.'

'Why? The only thing you're likely to pass are a couple of stray sheep. If you like, I can drive back to your house with you, make sure you get home safe and sound.'

Laura wildly thought that *safe and sound* were not words that she would naturally associate with being in his presence. *Unsafe* and *at risk* would have been nearer the mark, as far as her pulse rate and blood pressure were concerned, at any rate.

'And how would you get back here?' She did her best to get her breathing under control, knowing that he was picking up on her flustered behaviour and drawing his own conclusions.

'Walk.' Alessandro shrugged.

'Hand-made Italian leather shoes aren't made for walking miles on country lanes.' She stood up, legs feeling like jelly, and with some alarm she watched as he followed suit, standing up as well and crowding her with his towering presence.

'These shoes would do what I tell them to,' Alessandro murmured.

Laura gripped the back of the chair and drew in a deep, steadying breath. 'Is that how it works for you?'

'What are you talking about?' He frowned, perched once more on the table so that they were now eyeball to eyeball. She had the most expressive face of any woman he had ever seen. Her eyes were wide and clear and her freckles were standing out against the waxy pallor of her skin. She was hot and bothered and there was no way she could hide it. He liked that. It made all those cool, ultra-beautiful models he had dated in the past seem like plastic dolls in comparison.

This was a living, breathing, one hundred per cent sexy woman.

'You always get your own way?'

'Would it be a bad thing if I told you that I did? Ninety-nine per cent of the time?'

'No wonder you're so…so…*arrogant*!' She could barely think straight and yet there he was, as cool as a cucumber, making her feel as though *she* was the one making a mountain out of a molehill! Her fingers itched to smack that self-assured gleam right off his face and her anger felt a lot safer than that disturbing pull towards him.

'What's arrogant about telling it like it is?' he asked softly, unruffled. 'And, by the way, you're extremely cute when you're angry. I have a feeling you don't get angry very often.'

Laura gritted her teeth together, not wanting to stay where she was but somehow unable to unglue her feet from the floor and walk away.

'I don't fancy you,' she said in a strangled voice, 'and I'm certainly not interested in having a fling!'

'You do fancy me, you know.'

'You're the most egotistic man I have ever met!'

'If you didn't,' he pointed out in an ultra-reasonable

voice, 'you wouldn't be glaring at me and spitting fire. If you didn't fancy me, what I just said to you wouldn't have got under your skin the way it has. You would have been mildly amused, mildly insulted, largely indifferent. You might even have accepted my company back to your house because you wouldn't have felt threatened.' He grinned, eyebrows raised. 'We could always solve this vexing situation by putting it to the test...' he murmured, as though suddenly hitting upon the perfect solution.

He didn't give her time to think. He couldn't. He was so close to her that he could smell the clean, flowery smell of whatever scent she was wearing, and that fragrant scent matched the scent of her hair. With just the slightest hint of provocation, he thought that he might take her right here, in the kitchen, on the kitchen table. His erection was bulging, painful, and it was even more painful when he imagined her cool hands on it, followed by her cool, cool mouth. Since when had he ever had such an X-rated imagination?

He had to kiss her.

Laura sensed his intent before his mouth descended. She raised her hands to ward him off, mentally prepared to shove him firmly away, but...

Something happened. He kissed her gently. When his tongue flicked to probe the moistness of her mouth, she stifled a whimper. Her whole body trembled against him. Somehow, she had closed the gap between them and she could feel his hardness throbbing against her, a flagrant indication of how turned on he was.

She curled her fingers into his shirt and tugged him towards her. Every nerve in her shameless body was shrieking in hot response. Her breasts felt heavy, her nipples tingled, wanting more than just this kiss.

'So...' Alessandro reluctantly set her back gently. For a few seconds she could barely focus through the daze but when she did, mortification washed over her in a tidal wave of pure, undiluted horror.

'I don't know what just happened there,' she whispered.

'Lust.'

'I…I want to go now…' She looked away but was still hyper-aware of him standing close to her, his warmth mingling with hers in an agonising reminder of the kiss they had just shared. She was mortally horrified to admit to herself that she wanted to be back in his arms, kissing him and being kissed by him.

'Why?'

'What does that *mean*?' Her eyes flashed as they tangled with his and the breath caught in her throat.

Lust.

Hadn't she learned her lesson? She'd fallen victim to lust before and look at where it had got her! Except when she thought about Colin she couldn't remember feeling anything like what she had felt just then. That kiss, which had been meant to *prove* something, to *prove* that she was attracted to him, had sent her soaring into some crazy place where she hadn't even been able to *think*!

Colin's approach had been stealthy, like a serpent in the grass. He had charmed her, dismantled her doubts and inhibitions. Alessandro had just…swept in like a conquering marauder, intent on plunder.

She didn't even approve of him! She didn't even like him. So how on earth had he managed to…steamroller through all the defences she had so carefully put in place after her catastrophe with Colin?

'You don't want to go. You want to run away. We both know that we could easily have ended up—'

'I don't want to talk about this,' she said tightly. 'It shouldn't have happened. In fact, it probably only did because I had that drink. I'm not accustomed to drinking shorts. I wasn't thinking straight!'

'Tut-tut. You don't really believe that, do you?'

'You can't just come here and take what you want because you're bored,' she said, drawing in a deep breath and finally meeting his gaze and holding it.

'Whoever said anything about being bored?' He still wanted to touch her, wanted to feel the softness of her body without the barrier of clothes. The dress might not have been an overcoat but it might as well have been.

Laura squeezed her arms tightly around her body. 'I'm not looking for a guy like you.'

'A guy like me?' was the first response that came to hand, even though, more appropriately, he could have told her that if she wasn't looking for a guy like him, then he, likewise, wasn't interested in her or anyone else finding him and thinking they'd hooked him.

He wasn't into the business of encouraging false hope. He shoved away the uneasy thought that he had already managed to tell her a hell of a lot more than he had ever dreamed of telling any other woman in his life before.

Circumstances.

'You're everything I disapprove of. I don't know what the problem is with your father but you don't even make an effort! In all these years you've never shown any interest in trying to get to know him! In finding out what his life here is like… Do you know that he was actually *excited* at the thought of you coming up here twice? Taking us out for dinner? He had a problem choosing the right tie!'

For a few seconds Alessandro was lost for words. He stood up and prowled through the kitchen before leaning against the kitchen counter.

She couldn't read his expression. Was there *uncertainty*

behind that glower? Surely not. Surely he wasn't someone who was *ever* uncertain.

'Don't be ridiculous,' he muttered, standing directly in front of her, legs spread squarely apart, fingers hooked into the waistband of his trousers.

'Don't tell me I'm being ridiculous!'

'I don't think it's possible for my father to get excited over my appearance here, especially given the circumstances surrounding it. Actually, I doubt it's possible for my father to get excited over anything to do with me.' His mouth twisted into a wry smile before he abruptly turned away, to say over his shoulder, 'It's an understanding we share. As few displays of emotion as possible. It works.'

'He was excited because you were showing some interest in his life here. You should be so grateful you have him,' she said quietly, to his averted back.

That had him turning round to look at her. 'I count my blessings every night before I go to sleep.'

Are you always sarcastic? Laura wanted to ask him. And then it struck her that everyone had their defence mechanisms. That was his. He wasn't just an arrogant bastard who was here to complete a mission that would make his life easier, even if it meant railroading Roberto into doing something he didn't want to do.

He was far more complex than that.

'I would give anything to have a parent,' she said wistfully, 'even one I didn't get along with.'

'That's because you're sentimental,' Alessandro responded deflatingly. 'I'm betting there are damp tissues all round whenever you watch a tearjerker at the movies.'

'Would anything change your mind as far as removing your father is concerned? Are you just sticking around so that you can size my grandmother up and make sure she's not going to nick the silver the minute your back's turned?'

Alessandro shrugged. 'I'm taking it as it comes.'

'But it's a good thing,' Laura mused thoughtfully, 'because you've had to actually put yourself out to integrate into your father's life.'

'Let's not dress this up, Laura. It's a two-way street.' He had no idea what was propelling him to unpick scabs that had hardened over the years. Neither could he work out how they had managed to digress from the topic of when and where they were going to do something about the chemistry burning between them. Which was a far more interesting topic for discussion.

She lowered her eyes and didn't say anything. Frustrating woman, Alessandro thought. Any other woman would have been pressing to continue the conversation. The slightest shred of confidential information being shared would have opened the door to all sorts of thoughts of *really getting to know him*...the *real* him...

But, then, this woman was different, wasn't she? She might be hellishly attracted to him, but that still didn't make him *her type*. And since he wasn't *her type*, she wasn't looking for a way in to him via trying to lead him down the path of touchy-feely conversation. She was probably away with the fairies right now, thinking sentimental thoughts about her past.

'I don't know my father,' Alessandro heard himself say through gritted teeth, 'because he's always made sure to be unavailable.'

'Unavailable?'

'I was brought up by a selection of hired help,' he pointed out neutrally. 'Some excellent nannies, it has to be said. I barely remember my father being around when I was a kid. He spent most of his time abroad. He even...' Alessandro laughed mirthlessly '...went on holidays without me. Not that I didn't enjoy everything that vast sums

of money could buy. I did. I had holidays few could dream
of…in the company of the reliable hired help. At seven I
was shipped off to the finest boarding school in the country and so the tale of our serviceable but distant relationship goes on…'

'I'm sorry.' Laura took a few steps towards him and
Alessandro, cursing himself for the ease with which the
natural fortress he had built around himself had been invaded, shot her a wolfish half-smile.

'Sorry enough to come to bed with me?' he murmured.
'Trust me when I tell you that I'm not at all against a
sympa—'

'Stop it!' White-faced, Laura looked at him with blaz-
ing eyes. Was that what it had all been about? Had that
unexpected crack in his self-assured, forbidding exterior
been a deliberate ploy to try to get her to sleep with him?

She remembered the way Colin had infiltrated himself
into her life, playing on her emotions and saying whatever
he thought she might want to hear. In retrospect, it had
been so obvious.

Was she so transparent that Alessandro Falcone was
ready to pull the same stunt?

She placed her hands firmly on her hips and glared at
him, seething. 'That was crude!'

Alessandro had the grace to flush. Yes, it had been,
and crude was something he had never resorted to in his
life before.

'My apologies.' He raked his fingers through his hair
and stared at her, and for a few seconds she was so taken
aback by the apology that she couldn't find anything to
say. 'You're right. It's getting late. You should go. What
was it my father said about your grandmother not wanting
you to be gallivanting all over the country?'

Released from the awkward situation, Laura hovered

for a few seconds. She licked her lips and noticed the way he absently followed that little gesture with his eyes.

He wasn't coming closer to her, not by an inch. In fact, she could almost feel him pulling away, distancing himself, but the *heat* was still there. She could feel it like something tangible and alive between them.

Of course it would be madness to even think about going there, but it still gave her a heady kick to know that he found her attractive and she didn't honestly think it was because he happened to be here, in the middle of nowhere, bored and restless.

She wanted to shove him in the same bracket as Colin because it somehow felt safer, but he wasn't Colin.

'So…' She unconsciously stepped a tiny bit towards him. She wasn't even aware that she was doing it.

'So? So what?'

She shrugged, mesmerised by the smouldering darkness of his eyes.

'You really shouldn't, you know…'

'Shouldn't what?'

'Kiss me the way you kissed me…hot and hard and urgent…and then pull away and wipe your lips and somehow try to make-believe that it didn't happen and if it did, it wasn't your fault…'

'I never—'

He overrode her feeble interruption in the same dangerously soft voice. 'And then, when I take a step back, look at me as though you'd love nothing more than for me to kiss you all over again. Is that what you want? For me to kiss you all over again? Would you like me to lock the kitchen door, sweep the glasses off the table and make love to you right there? With the lights on so neither of us misses a thing?'

A thousand erotic images flashed through Laura's head.

Her mouth went dry and she knew that her whole body was aroused beyond belief. Moisture was dampening her underwear, pooling between her legs. It was somehow all the more of a turn-on because he was still keeping his distance. She felt giddy.

'No...' she managed, in a voice she didn't recognise.

'Sure? Because if you do...just say the word...'

'I've had one narrow escape when it comes to flinging myself into something...something...wrong...'

Alessandro shrugged. 'Like I said, there would be no wrongs or rights, because I'm not in it for the long haul.' Her body was so exquisitely provocative, especially as she seemed oblivious to that. He was holding himself back by sheer willpower but he had to. There was no way he intended to coerce anyone into bed with him, even if he knew that she wanted him.

She either came to him or she didn't.

His eyes darkened when he contemplated the possibility of her walking away. If he ended up being denied the promise of touching and making love to that glorious body, which he couldn't seem to get out of his head, he would have to instil a rigid regime of cold showers.

Never had the outcome of any encounter with any woman been so precariously balanced and he wondered whether that was why he could scarcely contemplate the thought of her turning her back on him for airy-fairy, woolly reasons that made no sense, because they were both adults and they both fancied each other. End of story.

'And I won't be using persuasive arguments to try to convince you that what we have needs to be...sated...'

'This is crazy!'

'When does your grandmother return from her holiday?'

'Huh?'

'We've covered the subject of sex,' he imparted with a

wave of his hand, 'so, before you go, I want to arrange a time and a place for me to meet her.'

Laura's brain seemed to be lagging behind. It seemed to have snagged somewhere between him asking her whether she wanted him to kiss her all over again and telling her that she just had to say the word.

Now he was moving on and that in itself said it all about the way he could compartmentalise sex, put it into a box that was quite separate from emotions or feelings or thoughts of the long-term.

She landed back down on earth and focused on him. 'Right. Yes. My grandmother.' Deep breath in, deep breath out. 'She's back on Friday. I'm going to pick her up from the airport. She could get a taxi back but, you know, she always thinks that taxi drivers are hell-bent on ripping her off by taking long, unnecessary detours...' She knew that she was babbling but she couldn't help it. And she wished he would stop looking at her like that, with his head ever so slightly inclined to one side, as though he was thinking all sorts of stuff that had nothing to with what she was talking about.

'In that case, Saturday. You and your grandmother can come here.'

'For tea? A drink?'

'Dinner. Maybe I'll do our digestive systems a favour and give Freya the evening off...fly my guy in. He could stay for the weekend.'

'Fly your guy in?'

'I have someone I can call on who cooks for me if I happen to eat at home.'

'Your father may have lots of money,' Laura said, 'but I don't think he would be happy with that situation.'

'No.' Alessandro gave her one of those slow, amused smiles that could knock her for six. 'I think he's so accustomed to Freya's challenged cooking that he might be confused if anything too edible came his way.'

'That's unkind.' She didn't want to, but he could bring a smile to her face without trying.

'Seven?' Alessandro asked, and she nodded.

Meeting her grandmother would be the last thing he would want to do when it came to finding out about the life his father would be leaving behind, the final piece of the jigsaw puzzle.

Laura couldn't imagine him kicking his heels in Scotland for much beyond that, even though he had sorted out an office for himself and appeared to be working quite efficiently.

'We'll be there.'

'No need for you to have arranged all this nonsense!' Roberto glared at his son from the stiff-backed chair where he sat, unhelpfully critical of the evening's arrangements.

'Don't you want me to meet the…ah…woman in your life?' Alessandro looked at his father and marvelled, yet again, at how simple conversation could end up feeling so tortured.

Not that strides forward hadn't been made. Ever since Laura had confided, a few days ago, about the dilemma with the tie, Alessandro had loosened up a little, had found it easier not to let his hackles rise after three seconds.

He had been invited to go over his father's company accounts and over dinner, the night before, they had actually managed a halfway decent conversation about the gradual sale of some of his father's interests now that he was fully retired.

Business was a safe topic of conversation and it was a damn sight more stimulating than the leaden silence that usually settled between them and to which they had become accustomed over the years.

'Old men don't have *women*.' Roberto adjusted his navy tie and eyed his gleaming shoes with a jaundiced eye. 'They have *companions*, my boy! Don't see why the sudden interest in meeting Edith anyway! Never had much time for what was going on in my life in the past!'

'But I wasn't trying to convince you to leave these goings-on before, was I?' Alessandro pointed out, because his father had developed an annoying and efficient habit of sweeping all talk of his move to London under the carpet.

'Must be missing your *women* in London...' Roberto said slyly. 'Must be hordes of 'em walking up and down outside your house, waiting for you to return... Nothing better to do with themselves, judging from the couple I met! Certainly couldn't get a job anywhere! Not with sawdust for brains!'

Alessandro, standing by the imposing Victorian fireplace, half smiled to himself because right now the last thing he was missing were women in London. Right now, this felt like a game and it was an exciting one. All he needed was the one woman right here on his doorstep, thank you very much.

'I'm doing just fine,' he murmured and missed the sharp look his father threw at him.

'Ever think of settling down?'

Alessandro looked at his father, shocked at this unexpected departure from their normal regime of polite conversation.

'Not if I can help it,' he said smoothly.

'You should,' Roberto grizzled. 'Marriage makes a man.'

Saved by the doorbell, Alessandro didn't get a chance to

quiz him on that because he had no idea what the quality of his father's marriage had been, but he could only assume that it had been a dictatorship in which his long-suffering mother had had to put up with the same sort of silent treatment from a man who had only spoken when absolutely necessary. He had a mental picture of two people moving around one another in silence.

Except...how much did he actually know for sure? He was about to answer the door to a friend in her twenties he had never known existed and a woman who was his father's girlfriend, someone else whose existence he had known nothing about.

Opening the front door, Alessandro dispelled the unsettling feeling of the floor shifting under his feet.

Laura had prepared her grandmother by telling her that Roberto's son wanted to meet her.

'I wondered when I'd get to meet him,' Edith had replied crisply. 'About time Roberto and his son sorted themselves out! Communication! That's all it takes!'

Laura had been too busy thinking her own thoughts to pay much attention to that remark.

What to wear? What did a girl wear when she was about to see a guy to whom she was stupidly attracted, a guy who had made her insides flip over with one kiss, a guy she most certainly did *not* want to have a fling with...

But was still driven to impress?

It was freezing cold outside but she wore a short-sleeved, deep blue, tight-fitting top with more of a plunging neckline than she would normally feel comfortable wearing and a long, black skirt with ballet pumps. Of course, she had to layer up and she could see her grandmother looking curiously at her dressy get-up, but it was no big deal. When someone invited you to dinner at their house, it was customary to show up in something other than jeans and a shapeless woollen jumper! She left her hair loose and it tumbled down her back, held back from her face with two blue clips on either side.

'Quite a picture,' her grandmother had said approvingly. 'Dress to impress?'

Which had almost made her take the whole lot off and climb back into her usual garb but she didn't and she was glad she hadn't when Alessandro opened the door and...

Black jeans, a faded black polo-neck jumper...he was so drop-dead gorgeous that her mouth went dry. She made sure not to look at him as they were ushered inside but she could feel his eyes on her as coats were removed and in just the tight top and her long skirt she was as conscious of the plunging neckline as she'd feared she might be.

'Fetching outfit,' Alessandro murmured, as Roberto and Edith walked towards the sitting room. 'Did you wear the top because you knew I wouldn't be able to take my eyes off you?'

'This old thing?' Laura said airily. 'I just stuck on the first thing in the wardrobe that came to hand.'

'What else is there in that wardrobe? I'm curious...'

'I told you that I'm not interested in...in anything... so...'

'I know.' He put both hands up in a gesture of mock surrender. 'You only kissed me because you had a couple of sips of gin and tonic and suddenly all your reservations were washed away! But I'm not your type because I'm an arrogant bore.'

'I never said you were boring.'

'So you find me scintillating company and as sexy as hell...it's almost impossible to keep your hands off me... but you're going to do your best to resist because some loser you met in London let you down.'

'This isn't the time or the place to be talking about this!' She looked surreptitiously at Roberto and her grandmother. Edith was doing a lot of talking and Roberto was laughing at something she had said. They were as absorbed in one another as a couple of teenagers on a first date.

'I like it. You can't run away. You never said what he did to you. Promised you the earth and then failed to deliver? Like I said, relationships are so much more straightforward when you lay down the boundary lines from the start.'

Laura stopped and looked up at him. 'He strung me along and I found out that it really wasn't going anywhere because he was married.' Remembered shame washed over her.

'What a class-A bastard,' Alessandro murmured softly. He looked down into those sea-green eyes and wanted to strangle the creep who had let her down. 'But you can't take that with you for ever and let it hang round your neck like an albatross.'

'I can learn from it.'

'Granted you can learn from it and then move on or else you can become so risk-averse that you never take a chance again.'

'I can reduce the odds by not having a stupid fling with someone who's totally unsuitable. I can wait until I meet the right guy for me. I don't think that's being risk-averse. I think that's being *sensible*!'

'Yes, but where's the fun in that?'

'It's not all about fun. When it comes to relationships, it's much more than having fun.'

'I bet your grandmother wouldn't agree. She looks a feisty lady. Should I ask her?'

'Don't you dare!'

She was so wrapped up in their conversation that she only noticed Roberto and her grandmother looking at them out of the corner of her eye, then she smiled a little faintly and cleared her throat.

'What's going on here?' Roberto tapped his way towards them and looked at both of them narrowly.

'Nothing,' Laura said.

'Good! Now, come along. No more of this hush-hush nonsense! Wasn't my idea to have a dinner party but now that it's happening, then into the sitting room you both go! No more standing out here and whispering! Bad damned manners!'

'Don't blame me!' Laura laughed and linked her arm through his. 'Blame your son!'

'Hope...' Roberto turned to look at Alessandro through narrowed eyes '...I won't have to.'

CHAPTER FIVE

HE WOULD LEAVE for the week and return on the weekend.
It made sense.

'Bloody waste of your time,' Roberto grumbled. 'Don't
see the point of it myself.'

'What's my choice?' Alessandro shrugged nonchalantly.
'Edith has returned the dinner invitation for next Saturday.
What's a polite guy like me supposed to do? She looks like
she might attack me with a rolling pin if I bail.'

'She's spirited, that one,' Roberto agreed.

'And we're getting nowhere with the decision about
London.' He had now spent more time solidly in the company of his father than he ever had in his life before, and
counting. At the rate he was going, he may as well import
his PA and set up camp for the long haul.

Time and big business waited for no man.

Strangely, though, he was missing the cut and thrust of
city life less than he had anticipated. Despite living in the
middle of nowhere, the broadband connection was fast and
for the past week he had established a routine that worked.

'London Schmondon,' his father contributed unhelpfully. 'More to life than pollution and smog.'

Stalemate.

But Alessandro was happy to take time out with this
particular stalemate situation.

Indeed, as he returned to Scotland the following Thursday, a couple of days earlier than anticipated, he was in high spirits. He could have travelled by helicopter but had instead chosen a first-class compartment on the train and had managed to get a considerable amount of work done. Few people kicked off before eight-thirty in the morning, by which time he was on his way, and by ten, when his phone began buzzing, he had already signed off two deals and had had his conference call to his people on the other side of the world.

By mid-afternoon he was at the closest station to the town and on the spur of the moment he set the satnav in the SUV he had conveniently left in the station car park to direct him to the school where Laura worked.

She would be finishing around now. She always stayed after close of day to mark books and get the classroom ready for the following morning.

Over dinner with her grandmother and his father he had told her that it sounded like a terminally tedious routine and then had enjoyed the way her cheeks had gone pink and her eyes had flashed. Even her *hair* had looked annoyed. She spent a lot of her time being annoyed with him, but underneath the annoyance ran a river of desire as strong as an ocean undercurrent. He'd never spent so much time dwelling on one woman, never mind a woman he hadn't taken to his bed. She was becoming a delicious obsession and he couldn't wait for the day when she came to him, when her defences had finally been broken down.

The school was perched at the edge of the village. Stepping out of the taxi, he spotted her car neatly parked in one of the spots for staff. It was just mid-afternoon, but the light was already fading fast and the playground, which was in front of the brick building, was empty of children.

This was the smallest school he had ever seen in his life and there was no way in unless you buzzed and announced yourself. So he buzzed and was let in by a middle-aged woman with rimless specs and a tightly pursed mouth after he explained that he was there to see Laura Reid.

'We all know who you are.' The woman's expression fell into a smile. Her pursed lips were obviously there to tackle any unwanted visitors to the school. 'Roberto's son. Maud at the post office bumped into the lady who does for Edith and she told us that you were here. You must be worried sick over the little turn your father had but he'll be right as rain in no time at all! Similar thing happened to my sister, bless her soul. Had a little stroke and then fell and broke her leg. She was off work for six months! And she bounced right back after that, so don't you go worrying unduly over your father. He's a robust one!'

All the time they were walking through a maze of corridors with classrooms on either side. It was bigger inside than it appeared from the outside. The walls were decorated with bright paintings and there was a low bookcase that ran the length of the corridor, stuffed with books.

He saw her before she noticed he was there. Straight from London and the wine bar, city crowds, he was knocked back at just how artless she was, sitting at her desk with a pile of exercise books on one side, frowning as she leaned over, marking. Her hair was escaping its ponytail, tendrils curling along her cheek, and she was absently chewing the top of her pencil.

'Thanks, I'll take it from here.' He smiled politely at the older woman who had shown him to the classroom and extracted his mobile from his pocket.

He stood to one side, slanting a glance through the small rectangular glass pane on the door so that he could just about see her, see her as she fumbled in her bag for her phone and then picked it up on the fourth ring.

'Just want to say,' he drawled, 'that chewing pencils

can be dangerous for your health...' He saw the way her face lit up, just for that split second when she recognised who was on the other end of the line, and he knew... She could push him away with one hand but she was beckoning him to come closer with the other. He felt the powerful kick of victory and it was an intensely satisfying sensation.

He pushed open the classroom door and she half stood, mobile phone still in her hand as she pressed the disconnect button. 'What are you doing here?'

That little frisson she had felt when she had heard his voice was gone. He could see from the tight expression on her face that she was going to do her best to just block him out because as long as she blocked him out she wouldn't have to deal with the sizzling chemistry between them.

And the harder she tried to block him out, the more he wanted to have her.

His eyes travelled the length of her, from tousled hair to fur-booted feet and then back up, noting the faded jeans and the bright red jumper.

'Thought I'd come a little earlier. So...this is where you work?' He looked around him and then strolled towards the pictures and essays that were tacked to the walls.

'Yes, it is,' Laura said tersely. She wanted to fling herself in front of the drawings he was inspecting with overdone interest because having him here, in the classroom, felt way too intimate. Or maybe it felt intimate because she'd been thinking about him. Correcting an essay while her mind had played and replayed that kiss. Even when he wasn't physically present, he could still manage to get under her skin and rattle her and she didn't like it.

'Nice. Homely.' He swung round to look at her. She was so determined to resist him. He felt that she would run for the hills if she only knew how much he relished the prospect of proving her wrong. As if either of them could resist what was between them.

'Why did you decide to come up here early?'

'A few things I wanted to run past you so I thought I'd see if you were still here. And you are. Why don't you stop...marking those books and have a coffee with me? There must be somewhere here we can go...is there?'

'I still have work to do.'

'Bring it with you. I can help you mark and then when we've finished we can have something to eat and I can talk to you about one or two things that have been on my mind.'

'Don't be silly,' she said, flustered. She smiled weakly past him at Evelyn, the deputy head, who was peering through the open doorway with lively curiosity. 'Just... er...'

'Yes, we met! Showed him in!'

Alessandro smiled at the woman who had ushered him to Laura's classroom and Evelyn blushed like a teenager.

'Perhaps,' he drawled, 'you could convince this stubborn little minx that she can leave with me so that I can take her out for a coffee...or something stronger...'

Laura didn't pay any attention to their bantering conversation but as soon as she and Alessandro were on their own, heading out to his car, she turned on him furiously.

'Thanks very much, Alessandro!'

'You're welcome. Next time you need rescuing from the monotony of marking books, feel free to call on me.'

'That's not what I was talking about!'

'No? Then you need to be a little clearer. I can't really follow you just going from your heated expression. Where's the quaint coffee shop? Or pub? I seem to remember that the town down the road is a little more vibrant when it comes to places to sit and pass the time of day.' He started the engine and began pulling out of the car park.

Was it his imagination or was the formidable middle-aged woman who had shown him in hovering by one of the windows?

'You don't come up here often,' Laura hissed, 'so you probably don't know just how fast the grapevine works!'

'Don't you get a little bored?'

'What are you talking about?'

'Sitting in a classroom, marking exercise books in a village that has twenty residents.'

'Are we back to your comments about it being a backwater? Because we just have to agree to disagree on that one.'

'Do you find it constricting, living with your grandmother?'

'Why would I?'

'Because you've lived on your own in London, had all the freedom you wanted. It might have suited you while you felt that Edith needed your presence, but she seems in full working order now, from what I've seen.'

'You didn't barge into my classroom so that we can discuss whether I enjoy living here with my grandmother or not.'

'So that's a no...you don't really enjoy it... What's that pub like? Any good?'

Laura glared at him. He was just so damned sure of himself! When she and her grandmother had joined him and Roberto for dinner, she had felt his dark, lazy eyes on her, as tangible as a caress, making her want to squirm, forcing her into awkward speech so that she stumbled over her words, blushing like a gawky teenager.

Had either her grandmother or Roberto noticed? She didn't know, and she had made sure to talk about him as little as she possibly could afterwards, even though her grandmother had asked leading, nosy questions.

'It's fine. Getting back to Evelyn—'

'Evelyn? Who's Evelyn?'

'The deputy head.'

'Never met the woman in my life before but, by all means, let's get back to her.' He pulled into a space, killed the engine and then relaxed back in the seat to look at her.

'She showed you to my classroom.'

'Ah. *That* lady… It took a while for her to crack a smile, but I sense an empathetic person. Remind me why we're talking about her?' The lights in the car park of the pub glinted off her vibrant hair, which was still in a ponytail. The expression on her heart-shaped face was cross and earnest. She had dragged a shapeless black coat over the red jumper outfit. It drowned her but that made no difference to her sex appeal. She still oozed it by the bucketload.

'She's going to wonder who you are.'

'She knew who I was. Someone had told someone who had told someone else who worked for your grandmother. It seems that I'm a talking point without even knowing it!'

Laura groaned. 'Lord knows what she's thinking.'

'Who knows what anyone's thinking?' Alessandro mused softly. He abhorred gossip but he had to admit that he was getting a certain buzz from this situation. 'Sometimes, though, it's easier. For instance, you must know what I'm thinking and here's what I think you're thinking…'

'I don't want to hear.' She looked at him and discovered that she couldn't look away. As fast as his image had crept into her head, she had done her best to dispel it by thinking about Colin and reminding herself that there was no point to learning curves if you just went ahead and ignored them the second they got a little inconvenient.

Colin had worked his charm on her, had used her own trusting nature against her, had played the part of the perfect boyfriend, and she had fallen for all of it, hook, line and sinker.

There was no way that she was going to jump headlong into a similar situation! Alessandro might be more upfront and more straightforward…he might call it *more honest*, but they were essentially made of the same stuff.

She had made a mental promise to herself that the next guy she got involved with would be a normal, considerate, one hundred per cent sincere and honest gentleman. The sort who didn't have a wife and a couple of kids stashed away in a house somewhere. Like Colin.

The sort who didn't change catwalk models as often as he changed his suits. Like Alessandro.

In fact, Alessandro posed a far more dangerous option. Which, frustratingly, was probably why she couldn't get him out of her head.

In fact, and this thought only now occurred to her, she had managed to clear her head of Colin with a lot more success than she was having trying to clear it of Alessandro.

Probably because she had been able to dump her job, dump London and disappear.

While with Alessandro…having made it his duty to avoid Scotland as much as possible, he now seemed to be on the scene all the time…like a guilty conscience.

'Would you like to hear what *I'm* thinking?'

'No!'

'Didn't think so. You'd much rather try to run away from what's between us.'

'There's *nothing* between us!' She was appalled at the edge of hysteria that had crept into her voice and she knew that he had heard it as well, if the knowing, speculative glint in his eyes was anything to go by.

No one could force her to do anything. She knew that. She wasn't going to let emotions or her body guide her actions. She had grown up since her unfortunate experience with Colin. She would use her head to make her choices! So why did she feel so hot and bothered as he continued to look at her with just the sort of pensive, amused speculation that she wished she could wipe off his face?

Why was it so terrifying to think of the way she was attracted to him? When, theoretically, she could control that attraction by boxing it up and ignoring its existence?

'Nothing except raw sexual attraction. You're cropping up in my head when I try to focus on work. It's very bad.'

'That's not my fault,' Laura said faintly, pushing down the little thrill she got from hearing him say that.

'Well, it's not *mine*.'

'There's *nothing* between us,' she repeated, just a little desperately, 'and I don't need the whole village gossiping about something that doesn't exist!'

'Ah, I get it. You think Evelyn the deputy head is going to start spreading unfounded rumours...'

'Yes!'

Personally, Alessandro could think of nothing worse than unfounded rumours. He'd had a couple of unfortunate experiences in that particular field...women who had stupidly spoken to a couple of reporters who had had nothing better to do than run an article or two on the private life of whatever billionaire they could find. They had intimated there had been more to their relationship than had actually been the case and had found to their cost that he could be ruthless when it came to eliminating complications. Women who expected more from him than he was willing to give became complications and women who thought that talking to reporters might somehow pin him down to something he didn't want invariably found themselves dispatched without delay.

Alessandro had never really thought about that side of

his life, the side that refused to become emotionally involved, but on the few occasions when it *had* crossed his mind he had concluded that it had to do with his background.

Love had not been readily shown. He assumed his father cared about him but with reserve and distance, and that reserve and distance had created in him an emotional vacuum that he had never chosen to explore or overcome.

He just wasn't one of those types in search of happy-ever-afters. He relied on what he knew and what he knew was the world of power and big money, the concrete world of business, of deals and machinations and running an empire.

Women were stress-busters. He was upfront with them and if some of them got the wrong idea or started imagining a future that wasn't on the cards, then whose fault was that? Not his. He was nothing if not scrupulously honest when it came to that sort of thing.

So unfounded rumours in a small village...?

He decided that this would be his exception to the rule. What she did to certain parts of his body was worth the inconvenience.

'Doesn't matter, though, does it? Considering they're unfounded?'

'That's not the point.'

'You don't care what people think to the extent that you'd actually pay attention to what they say about something that doesn't even exist, do you?'

Laura met those dark, cynical eyes evenly. 'Yes, I would, because I actually care what people think of me.'

'Why?' Alessandro was genuinely mystified.

'Why don't *you*?'

'Come again?'

'It's not natural to not care *at all* what anyone thinks

of you. Okay, I get it that you don't care what a perfect stranger thinks of you or what you choose to do. I mean, if the milkman peers past you into your hallway and doesn't like your choice of wallpaper, it's no big deal. But don't you care what *anyone* thinks of you or what you do? Isn't there *anyone* whose opinion matters to you?'

'Shall we continue this fascinating conversation over a very early glass of wine?' He reached across to open the car door on her side and his forearm brushed against her breast. He felt her flinch back and half smiled, even though he was still playing around with the annoying question she had posed.

Aside from the gruelling demands of his job, what did he care about? And was not caring a strength or a weakness? Irritated by this sudden bout of introspection, he swept it aside and levered his big body out of the car.

Enthusiastic to be in his company she most certainly was not. Tales of big, bad wolves sprang to mind, with him in the starring role of the big, bad wolf.

Suddenly, it didn't seem as amusing to tease her as it had done minutes before.

Hell, she really cared about what sort of reputation she would get from just being seen with him! They'd done nothing and it was still bugging her.

He toyed idly with the idea of telling her that it was better to be hung for a sheep than a lamb. If the entire village had nothing better to do than twitch their net curtains and speculate, then why not give them something to speculate about?

'You're not trying to run away from an awkward conversation, are you, Alessandro?' She fell into a brisk walk to keep pace with his longer strides.

Wherever he had come from, it hadn't been from sitting behind a desk. He must have changed in his luxurious penthouse apartment before heading up. He oozed casual sex appeal in jeans and a jumper over which he was wearing a mega-expensive trench coat. When it came to practicality in cold Scottish weather, it scored a zero, but in terms of looking indecently good, it was a ten with room to spare.

'I've never run away from anything in my life.' He held the door open and she ducked under his arm. 'And definitely not from idle, wagging tongues, but if you prefer, I'll make sure I keep a healthy distance. What would you like to drink?'

Laura breathed a sigh of relief that the pub was relatively empty and as it wasn't in the village there was less chance of her being recognised, although wasn't Alessandro right? Why should she care? She had cared so much about what had happened with Colin that she had packed her job in without thinking of the repercussions. She could have taken some time off, genuinely because her grandmother had needed her, and then returned to her job, not caring that she might bump into Colin, because he was a bastard so why should she? Not caring if some of her colleagues might have suspected what had been going on, because they hadn't been her close friends so their opinion mattered but within reason.

She could have remained in London because... Living here was fine but there were times when she did feel as though time had been frozen and she wasn't moving forward. She could have quit her job and gone into teaching, but in London...

No. She did *not* want to start thinking of what-ifs and if-onlys!

'A cup of tea would be nice.'

'Tea? It's almost five-fifteen. We can have a glass of wine. I won't tell if you don't...'

She smiled nervously at him but before she could work

out a suitable negative response he was heading towards
the bar, where the young girl serving behind the counter
dropped what she'd been doing and flew over to take his
order.

However cool and detached he was with his father, and
however forbidding he could be when he chose to, he could
certainly pull the charm out when it suited him, Laura
thought wryly. The poor girl could hardly pour the wine
into the glasses and she was beetroot red.

'So there's a reason I decided to come up here early and
pay you an unexpected visit.' He angled his chair away
from her so that he could stretch out his long legs.

His voice was brisk and businesslike. He was keeping a
healthy distance between them. She could have been at an
informal job interview! Perfect, she thought with a twinge
of treacherous disappointment, because his flirting was
stupidly addictive.

'Aside, that is, from wanting to see where you work...'
He grinned and then steepled his fingers to his lips. 'But
starting with Edith...'

'Are you going to tell me that you think she's after your
father for his pot of gold?' Laura bristled. She wondered
whether she would stop being so attracted to him if she
could somehow maintain a state of permanent low-level
anger. If she was *angry* with him, then she couldn't be *attracted* to him, could she?

Sometimes, though, it was impossible to respond to him
the way her head told her to. Sometimes he just got under
her skin and no amount of rubbing could get rid of him.

'Actually, I happen to like your grandmother very
much,' Alessandro admitted seriously. 'I don't know what
I expected but she...she seems good for my father...'

'And what did you expect?'

'Someone a little more subservient. I'll be honest, my father isn't the easiest of men. I didn't envisage that he would be…attracted…God, have I really said that?…attracted to someone as outspoken.'

'What was your mother like?'

'That remains one of life's mysteries. It's not a subject I have ever discussed with my father and it isn't a subject I intend discussing with you.' He'd tried with his father and had come up against a brick wall of uncooperative evasiveness. He'd stopped trying a long, long time ago.

Laura blushed. His voice had cooled. Sexual innuendo and flirting was fine. A serious conversation apparently wasn't. Whatever he did, he did on his terms and that included how much he wanted to share of himself.

Not that it mattered. This wasn't a show-and-tell, getting-to-know-you session.

'She keeps him in line.' Laura smiled. 'They suit one another. She likes fussing over someone and he enjoys being fussed over. She tells him what he should and shouldn't do and he's like a little lamb when he's with her.'

'I can't believe we're talking about the same person. No matter, the point is…I may possibly have got it wrong when I decided that the only option was to move my father to London.' He sipped some wine and looked at her over the rim of his glass. He really enjoyed the way she was so transparent, so lacking in artifice. 'I hadn't thought that the life he had built here for himself was so… Well, put it this way, I hadn't thought that he'd built *any* life for himself here. It seems that I was wrong and I'm big enough to admit it.'

Laura couldn't help it. She rolled her eyes heavenwards and Alessandro frowned.

'Oh, honestly!' She sighed and laughed lightly, taking in his bemused expression. 'Hasn't anyone *ever* rolled their eyes or clicked their tongue at something you've said?'

'I've just admitted that I may have been wrong. What's the rolling of the eyes all about?'

'You're *big* enough to admit it? What was the other option? That you carry on pretending that he's a lonely old man and drag him down to London rather than admit you'd got it wrong? We *all* misjudge situations once in a while.' He was staring at her with a blank expression and she realised that didn't apply to him. That just wasn't how his world worked. In Alessandro's world misjudging of situations didn't happen but, then, his world was all about stuff that could be measured. Deals, money, business…things that were a million miles away from emotions, feelings and lives, things where misjudgement happened all the time. 'Okay,' she said slowly, 'so now you've recognised that, what happens next?'

'He still needs to move out of that oversized mansion. I always wondered why he bought it in the first place. I am prepared to admit that remaining here might be for the best. The hunt will have to begin to find him somewhere a little more compact, a little more manageable…'

'Aren't you going to discuss this with your father?'

'I'll broach the topic. So…now that's out of the way, let's talk about the weekend.'

'I'm not going anywhere with you.' She couldn't give in to his flirting. She couldn't let herself be overtaken by something as stupid and transitory as physical chemistry. She bristled at the thought that he felt he could just try to dictate how she should spend the little amount of time he designated to spending in a backwater he normally wouldn't be caught dead in. She tried to rustle up Colin's image in her head but all she could see were Alessandro's far too knowing dark eyes focused on her with the sort of lazy intent that sent her nervous system into frantic overdrive.

'I realise that there's some sort of physical attraction between us. I'm not going to deny that, but that doesn't mean that either of us has to succumb to it and, furthermore, it's insulting to think that you just come here and then feel that you can take what you want, never mind the consequences!' She lowered her voice to a meaningful hiss. 'You can't!'

Alessandro inclined his head to one side and the infuriating man didn't say anything.

She looked at her wine glass and realised that it was empty. How had that happened? She rarely drank unless she was out and certainly never at this crazy hour of the evening!

'So you may think you're some kind of saint who can wash his hands of relationships just because you've been kind enough to warn those poor women you date that you're not in it for longer than a couple of days...'

'Hmm... Days... Even for me that would be a rapid turnover.'

Laura ignored him. 'But I'm not one of those women!'

'I never thought that you were.'

'Because I don't happen to be a six-foot-three catwalk model?' she asked bitterly. She had felt so desirable when he had kissed her...nothing had prepared her for the onslaught of lust that would wipe out all her inhibitions as though they had never existed.

But, then, the guy was a force to be reckoned with when it came to the art of seduction. One look at him would tell you that.

'Because I've never had to employ such restraint with any woman in my life before.'

'Well, that may be but it certainly doesn't mean that I'm going to spend the weekend accommodating you!' She tilted her chin at a stubborn angle and glared at him.

'I think you're getting all hot under the collar for no reason,' Alessandro said mildly.

'And I disagree!'

'I wasn't trying to arrange a convenient time to wage an assault on your maidenly virtue, tempting though that option is…' He stared off into the distance, as though wrapped up in all sorts of pleasant thoughts, and then shook his head ruefully. 'I was actually about to say that the weekend might be a good time to start trying to consolidate some of my father's possessions in preparation for a move, should he agree, of course.'

'Oh.'

'Disappointed?'

Laura wanted the ground to open up and swallow her whole. No wonder he was sitting there grinning at her! 'Relieved,' she snapped.

'Good! I will talk to my father this evening and who knows…something might well be sorted out before I leave.'

And once sorted, his life would, of course, return to its normal hectic pace within the confines of his own comfort zone in London.

Or…

He gazed at her flushed face thoughtfully.

Maybe not. The last thing he needed was to leave behind unfinished business…

CHAPTER SIX

'Downsize? What's the point of *that*? Not one for living in a rabbit hutch!'

Alessandro remained silent. His loose-limbed posture in the chair facing Roberto smacked of utter relaxation. Only the stillness of his body betrayed his awareness of the fact that, as always, nothing was going to be easy when it came to his father.

But, for once, he had converts to his cause. Laura and her grandmother had insisted on sitting in on the meeting with his father in a show of moral support, even though Alessandro had told them that it wouldn't be necessary.

'He can be a stubborn old fool,' Edith had announced, as soon as she had been told of Alessandro's decision and given it the green light. Not, Alessandro thought, that a green light from anyone was required, but Edith was not a woman any sane person would pick a fight with. 'Digs his heels in and refuses to budge. Won't be able to pull that one on me, though! I can be a stubborn old fool as well!'

Alessandro had shrugged and so, later that evening, they had all headed up to the manor house, like gunslingers galloping into town to confront the local bad boy.

'And don't...' Roberto wagged his finger at Edith a little later '...you start telling me that you agree with that son of mine!'

'You put that finger away,' Edith said in a clipped voice.

'That son of yours is right and you know it! Who was it who told me not four months ago that he found walking from the kitchen to the bedroom "*a bloody chore*"? And I'm quoting a certain person here. He's sitting not a million miles away, being a stubborn old fool, as I knew he would be!'

Alessandro shot Laura a sideways glance, caught her eye, kept looking until she looked away and then settled down for the count.

It was nearly six-thirty. Yet another unappetising dish prepared by Freya was bubbling away merrily in the oven and in a few minutes he would fetch a chilled bottle of wine, which he decided would be an excellent accompaniment to the thrilling battle of wills unfolding in front of him.

He already knew what the outcome would be. His father might be able to argue for England but he would never be able to hold out against a determined Edith. The woman had missed her calling as a riot-control specialist in a prison block.

At the moment she was reminding Roberto of every conversation they had ever had in which he had complained about the size of the house. There had been a lot, especially in recent months, and she had a very good memory.

'And don't you even bother telling me that you can always live in one wing of the house! Stuff and nonsense!'

'You're a harridan, woman! A harridan!'

'And then there's that garden so-called of yours! How big is it, exactly? Ten acres? What's a man of your age doing with ten acres of garden? You'd need a car to get round the lot! I'll wager you haven't been to the lavender field since last year! And who told me that the greenhouse was getting a little out of control? You won't let any of the gardeners in to tend the plants but you can't tend them all on your own, admit it!'

Alessandro looked at his father's scowling face with amusement. He wore the harried look of someone who'd just found a hole in his defences and simultaneously discovered that he lacked the time and the necessary tools to do a patch-up job.

He had never seen Roberto on the back foot. His father had always made a show of being in command. He had been a towering, forbidding and silent figure in Alessandro's childhood, a largely absent one during his teenage years and a broodingly taciturn and borderline belligerent one as Alessandro had reached adulthood.

That was not the same man sitting in the burgundy covered chair now, glowering at Edith before huffing into silence.

'You're a damned witch, woman!' He looked at her and then said slyly, 'Could you have an ulterior motive for trying to get me out of this house? I hear that house down the road from you is coming up for sale in the next month or so… You know the one I mean…those layabout softies from Edinburgh inherited it when old man Saunders died. Wouldn't fancy getting your hands on me, would you?'

'You should be so lucky!'

'If you'll excuse me…' Alessandro stood up, flexed his muscles '…I'm going to get some wine and, Laura…' he shot a glance at her, eyebrows raised '…why don't you accompany me? You can check on whatever delight Freya's shoved in the oven for us to eat. It's been in there for the past four hours so whatever it's meant to be it'll probably emerge as baby food.'

'Don't you go thinking you've won this round, young man!' Roberto banged his walking stick on the parquet flooring and glared at his son. 'Won't be browbeaten into doing what I don't want to do and…' he transferred his beady eyes to Edith, who wore the smug expression of the victor '…won't be nagged into it, either!'

Alessandro shrugged and left the room with the vague promise that the matter could be revisited over dinner. Behind him, Laura followed. She hadn't said a word, leaving her grandmother to argue with Roberto. She had sat in her chair, her body rigid with tension, her focus exclusively on Roberto, but she had been aware of his son with every pore in her body. Alessandro had relaxed back in the chair, his fingers lightly entwined on his stomach, his legs outstretched and loosely crossed at the ankles. She had sensed his alertness, his watchfulness… Her antennae had picked it up like a gazelle picking up the scent of a jungle cat.

'I think,' he drawled the minute they were in the kitchen, 'that what we have in there is called a foregone conclusion. Maybe we should leave your grandmother to seal the deal and mop up the blood before we take the wine in. I can't believe she got the better of my father! Memorable.' He poured them both a glass of Chablis and watched as she went straight to the oven, removed whatever was being cremated in a cast-iron casserole pot, winced and then rested the pot on the hotplate.

She was doing her best to avoid eye contact. Even when she took the glass of wine from him, those apple-green eyes skittered away hurriedly.

For a few seconds she remained hovering before subsiding into one of the kitchen chairs and taking a long gulp from the long-stemmed glass.

'It would have broken my grandmother's heart if your dad left to live in London. I mean, I know Roberto is probably fond of this place, I know he's lived in it for…well, for as long as any of us can remember, but I think he knows deep down that it's far too big for him. Would you like me to find out whether the cottage at the end of the village will be coming up for sale?' She risked a nervous glance at Alessandro, who was perched against the kitchen counter, staring at her with just the sort of *concentration* that could send her pulse flying to the four winds.

'No need.'

'What do you mean?'

'If you give me the names of whoever owns the place, I'll take it from there.'

'But you won't know who they are and they don't actually live in the cottage. I believe it's a brother and sister. I remember chatting to them when they came to Jim's funeral.' She grimaced. 'They couldn't wait to leave. Since then they've been down a couple of times to make sure the cottage is still standing but they haven't done anything with it and I'm sure they won't be interested in moving in.'

'I just need the names. What's the boy called?' He reached for his mobile and tapped in the name given to him.

'What good is that going to do?'

'I'll get in touch with him.'

'But what if he doesn't want to sell? I know you think that this is just a backwater, but it's possible that they might want it as a holiday home. It's absolutely stunning in the summer months and the salmon fishing is very good…'

'He'll sell because I'll make him an offer he can't refuse. If he wants a holiday home in this part of the world, he can buy one somewhere else. I intend striking while the iron's hot. Give my father a little time to start working on another argument for staying put and I could find myself in the same position as I'm in now this time next year.'

'And that would never do, would it?' Laura said tartly.

'Having to drag yourself away from hectic city life to go through the horror of repeat trips to the backwater?'

Alessandro smiled slowly at her. He sipped some of the wine and carried on looking over the rim of the glass, liking what he saw. Jeans, a checked shirt peeping out from behind a dull red jumper. The same fur-lined boots she had been wearing in the classroom. High fashion wasn't going to be staging a takeover any time soon with her and he really liked that. He also liked the way her skin was tinged pink, the way she was mutinously doing her best to meet his eyes and hold them, the way she didn't wear any make-up so that the sprinkling of freckles across the bridge of her nose stood out against her pale, smooth skin. Her hair wasn't in a ponytail but she had still pulled it back into a single long braid, which she had pulled over her shoulder, and it was tied at the end with a red piece of stretchy elastic.

What was a man to do? he wondered.

She wasn't one of his catwalk models, who were as hard as nails and knew the score before they jumped into bed with him.

She was also nursing a broken heart, although, as far as he was concerned, after a year and a half the heart should not only be mended but would benefit from some energetic exercise. The sort of exercise he was an expert at providing.

And how complicated could it get? They lived in opposite ends of the country and he knew, unerringly, that although she fancied him, she would never look for anything lasting with someone of whom she fundamentally disapproved.

And vice versa. She might make a great change from his predictable diet, but she was as poles apart from him as he was from her. They could have come from different planets and he couldn't wait to explore their differences.

A big plus was that it would make visiting his father a thing of anticipation, at least for a while. Of course, denial would be a safer option because she didn't obey the rules of the game he played when it came to women, but denial was something with which he had little experience. What was the point? When it came to sex, all was fair in love and war between consenting adults. And her consent was simmering just below the surface. He could sense it.

'City life *can* be hectic,' Alessandro agreed. 'Maybe I've been viewing these trips to Scotland in entirely the wrong light.' He glanced around at the kitchen as though pondering whether there was more to it than met the eye, maybe a magic wardrobe concealing a lion and a witch, and then he gazed at her with his head tilted to one side. 'For *backwater*, one can always read *peaceful*. Maybe I haven't thoroughly explored the potential for kicking back here.' He shrugged, still giving the matter some thought. ''Course, my father's endearing ways might have detracted from the temptation to spend longer than a few minutes in the place but I sense we might be getting onto a different footing...'

'You do?' Laura subdued a brief flare of thrilling anticipation at the prospect of him being around, which she immediately squashed, choosing to interpret the way her heart skipped a beat as nothing more than perfectly understandable satisfaction that father and son might manage to work their way to a better relationship.

'He has friends and a social life here,' Alessandro mused, 'so I'm thinking that there might be more to him than has always met the eye. Once or twice I've even caught a flash of humour in something he's said and I've always thought that humour was something he disapproved of on principle. And, of course, I've seen first-hand that he's not as intransigent with the entire human race as I've always been led to believe. Your grandmother knows how to wield a big stick and he obeys. Doesn't take a genius to work out who wears the trousers in that relationship.'

'Roberto is all bark and no bite.'

'I wouldn't go so far as to say that…'

Laura looked at him curiously and he returned her gaze with raised eyebrows. 'I've discovered he has a healthy set of teeth. Trust me. But…' he shrugged and slanted her a crooked smile '…I don't get away much. Might do me good to discover what this part of Scotland has to offer.'

'Why don't you get away much? Don't you enjoy going on holiday?' Laura couldn't fathom why anyone who was as rich as Alessandro didn't feel the urge to take time out. He could afford to go anywhere on the planet.

'Come again?'

'You said you don't get away much. Why not? Surely you must get tired of working all day, every day, without let-up? Your father says you never stop. He tells me that you're always in the newspapers about closing some big, important deal or other. Doesn't it all get a little too much?'

'How would my father know about deals I've closed?' Alessandro queried silkily.

'Because he has a scrapbook of newspaper cuttings.'

Sudden silence filled the room, then Alessandro swirled his glass and finished the remainder of the wine. Scrapbook? What scrapbook? Since when?

'I don't take holidays because I don't have time,' he told her bluntly. He thought of the houses he owned, one in the Caribbean, another in Paris, a third in Tuscany. Aside from the occasional business trip to Paris, when he occasionally might stay in his apartment there, they remained vacant, tended by paid help, waiting in readiness for the day he decided he could take the time off.

He brought the conversation neatly back to the matter in hand, clearing his head of a sudden onslaught of uncustomary confusion when he thought of those unused holiday homes, slowly maturing as good investments but never enjoyed, when he thought of his action-packed, high-pressured life that never allowed him time to sit back and take a break. 'Which is why it might work to come here a little more often than I have done in the past.' He strolled towards her, wine bottle in one hand, filling his glass as he walked. He didn't sit down, however. Instead, he chose to stand right next to her, which immediately made her feel as though she was suffocating. 'Of course, it would help if I had someone to show me around...'

'Someone to show you around?'

'I only know my father's house and whatever lies within the radius of about three miles. Even when I used to return here from boarding school, I never bothered to explore the countryside.'

Laura's brain was lagging behind. Who did he have in mind to show him around?

As if she couldn't guess. She felt a frisson of excitement ripple through her. He was so close to her that she had to look up at him and when she dipped her eyes...

Her mouth went dry.

'You should have,' she said faintly. 'It's worth exploring. Maybe we should return to the sitting room.' She pushed back her chair and managed to squirm out of it without coming into contact with his far-too-big, far-too-dominant and far-too-powerful body. 'Roberto has very strict eating times. In a second, my grandmother will fly in here and start fussing over the food.'

'Maybe she could transform it into something edible.'

Alessandro stood aside, allowing her the distracted change of topic, because sooner rather than later he would return to the matter in hand. 'Although that might require a skilled magician.'

They returned to the sitting room to find Edith and Roberto poring over an illustrated gardening book that she had brought back from Glasgow as a present, and there was a jaunty tie resting on the coffee table next to him.

Alessandro looked at the tie, caught his father's eye and was gratified when his father reddened.

'Silly woman insisted on bringing me back this tie,' he muttered while Edith looked at him with open affection. 'Can't imagine where an old man like me is going with a yellow tie with red birds on it!' He picked it up and absently placed it over the navy blue tie he was currently wearing, and Edith beamed.

'And now…' she slapped her thighs briskly '…that everything is sorted and this stubborn father of yours has seen the sense in downsizing, it's time to feed him!'

It was a little after nine-thirty when Alessandro delivered both Laura and Edith back to their house and it had been, for the first time in living memory, a rewarding evening.

At least insofar as the downsizing decision went. Roberto had capitulated to his fate in style. He now knew exactly the sort of place he was looking for and unless the Saunders place filled each and every single requirement, they could damn well go jump.

Alessandro was quietly determined that it would, whatever the cost. Speed was of the essence and he would move quickly. Money talked and he had a lot of it.

'So…' That was his opening word, when Edith had finally retired to bed and Laura was showing him to the door as though she couldn't get there fast enough. 'You never answered my question.' Alessandro leaned against the door frame and looked at her.

Her heart fluttered. 'What question?'

'I'm going to be here for the next few weekends at the very least. I might even split my time until this whole house business has been sorted out. Are you going to be my tour guide while I'm here?'

Laura glanced over her shoulder towards the staircase. Her grandmother had retired with her cup of hot chocolate but there was no telling whether she would reappear without warning and she didn't want Edith's curiosity aroused.

Because there was nothing to be curious about.

Yet...

That treacherous thought slipped into her head without warning and she shivered with forbidden excitement.

'You don't need a tour guide, Alessandro,' she replied, buying time, hating herself for being tempted. 'You've got a car. You can drive yourself around and take in all the sights...'

'But it wouldn't be nearly as much fun, would it?' he said softly.

Their eyes tangled and slow, burning colour crawled into her cheeks.

'What are you so scared of?' he asked. He could see the little pulse beating in the side of her neck, an indication that the cool, composed voice did not reflect what was going on inside her. But he knew what was going on inside...he had felt it in that sizzling, shared kiss.

'I'm not scared!'

'And you keep glancing up the stairs. Do you think your grandmother is pressed to the floor of the bedroom with a glass so that she can eavesdrop on whatever we might be saying?'

'Of course not,' she said uncomfortably. But who knew when it came to her grandmother?

'I'm attracted to you.' Alessandro didn't move an inch closer to her but it *felt* as though he had. It *felt* as though he had caressed her and left a scorching trail behind on her skin. 'And you're attracted to me...'

Laura opened her mouth to protest but she remained silent because to deny it would be to deny the obvious.

'That doesn't mean anything.' She risked a quick look at his dark, handsome, serious face. 'It would be stupid to do anything about that.' She was aiming for dismissive. Instead, she ended up with a nervous squeak. 'Life is about choices,' she continued, clearing her throat. 'I chose the wrong guy when I was in London and I'm not going to repeat my mistake.'

'You will only climb into bed with a man who promises to put a ring on your finger? What if he never comes along?'

'Then I guess I'll end up on my own.'

Alessandro didn't say anything. He had never been rebuffed by any woman and her refusal fired him up like a challenge he now knew he had no intention of resisting.

'My father's possessions will need to be packed up.'

'Huh?' Was that it? She felt unjustly deflated. Her body was still throbbing, as though he had physically touched her. So what was wrong with being careful? Why wasn't she more relieved that he wasn't going to pursue an attraction neither of them had asked for? And how was it that he had somehow managed to make her feel like an unadventurous bore?

'I intend to get the ball rolling on this one first thing in the morning.' Alessandro straightened and opened the front door, letting in some freezing wintry air. 'I'll have to have a look at the place before I make a decision but

I'm hoping that there won't be any gaping construction black holes.'

'Of course.' Her mind was still in a whirl, thinking about the way he had told her that he was attracted to her, as if sexual attraction was the most natural thing in the world, as if acting upon it was a no-brainer.

'Once that's sorted, I can arrange for work to begin on reconfiguring it to my father's exacting standards. In the meanwhile, you probably know more than I do about what personal items will need boxing and what can be left for the removal men.'

'It's moving a bit fast, isn't it?'

'I've never seen the point of delaying the inevitable. And while this is going on, I intend to stay put, make sure that there are no unfortunate hitches.' He paused and looked down at her upturned face. He itched to smooth his hand over her cheek, cup her face, pull her so close that she would be able to feel exactly what she did to his body. 'Would your school be able to release you for a couple of days so that you can help with the packing of my father's things? I have no idea where he keeps anything and even less interest in finding out. I will also have to work while I'm here...'

'I can't just take time off! They need me there.'

'And I need you here.'

The way he said that, in a slow, lazy drawl, imbued the remark with all sorts of delicious, dark innuendo.

'I can't trust outsiders to handle my father's personal possessions, whatever they might be, and he hasn't got the energy to do it himself.'

'Perhaps you ought to see whether the house is going to be available or not first,' Laura said, transfixed by the little smile playing at the corners of his mouth.

'If I want it to be available, then it will be available.

And I want it to be available. When can you let me know about taking time off?'

'I... Okay, I'll talk to Evelyn, see what she says, whether they can spare me for a day or so. I can't promise anything.'

'If you like, I can talk to her. I'm sure I could convince her to release you from your chains for a few days.'

'A few days?'

Alessandro shrugged nonchalantly. 'Who can tell? I have no idea how much my father owns and how much needs packing up. It could be a handful or a vanload.'

Laura thought that if he spoke to Evelyn she would probably let her have the rest of the term off. The man was too charming, too persuasive, too damned sexy for his own good. He was the personification of danger, but instead of backing away from him she stayed where she was, rooted to the spot, mesmerised against her will.

He fancied her, found her attractive...

It felt as though he was something exciting, exotic, unbearably tempting...blown in on distant winds, turning her protected world on its head and making her wonder how long she would hide away in this small village with her grandmother, making her wonder if all this self-protection was really worth it.

She had fled London and had welcomed the soothing balm of being back in Scotland. Her grandmother's temporary frailty had been a distraction and then she had busied herself applying for the teaching job and familiarising herself with the school and the pupils. She had congratulated herself on having a new life and leaving behind a miserable situation. She had told herself that it was better to lead a quiet, contented, uneventful life than one in which she ended up being hurt. She would never be hurt again. She would never *allow* herself to be hurt again.

But had she been *living*?

Alessandro made her question her resolutions. Going to London in the first place had been a huge adventure for her, then Colin had appeared on the scene and everything had gone pear-shaped. She had obeyed her first instinct to run away, back to safety.

Anyone else might have just seen that as an obstacle to be surmounted. She was only twenty-six and he hadn't been the great love of her life, as time had revealed! Anyone else would have carried on, trusting that the next adventure would turn out a bit better.

Instead, she had retreated and she now wondered whether that hadn't become part of her make-up over time. Had the loss of her parents made her fearful? So careful that it had become a handicap? And was that fearfulness going to follow her for the rest of her life?

Alessandro, with his dark, sinful temptation, made her question the choices she had made.

What would happen if she accepted the gauntlet he had flung at her feet? Would she go up in flames? Would the world stop turning?

Of course not!

But maybe she would be able to re-enter the world without wearing so much protective garb around her that she could barely move, never mind live. She couldn't let one poor experience blind her to what life had to offer, could she?

And Alessandro, in a weird way, might pose a danger because she was physically attracted to him, but physical attraction was like a virus that struck hard and then blew over—in another way, he couldn't have been a safer bet. He wasn't luring her on with the pretence of a relationship, as Colin had. And she was never going to fall for him. The guy for her really would be someone who shared her beliefs and values and wasn't motivated by money and power.

'Are you going to carry on staring at me? Or shall we move the conversation along?'

Laura started and reddened. 'I'll get the time off, although I'm not sure myself where his possessions are kept. I mean the ones he wouldn't want a team of removal men to manhandle, and I'm sure he'll insist on doing it himself. He's very proud. Doesn't like accepting help.'

'You knew where to find a scrapbook.' Alessandro clenched his jaw and shoved his hands into his trouser pockets. For a second his formidable self-control seemed to desert him but it was only a fleeting sensation, then he met her green eyes squarely. 'I expect,' he told her drily, 'the rest of his stuff might be in the same cubbyhole. People are nothing if not predictable.'

'It wasn't in a cubbyhole. It was in his bedside drawer. I went to fetch some tablets for him shortly after his operation. It fell out. Maybe he'd been looking through it.'

Alessandro didn't want to feel any softening towards his father. The time for that had come and gone years and years ago. He knew Roberto Falcone for what he was, an unforgiving man who had probably never wanted a child in the first place, a man who kept his past a secret, even though, as a kid, Alessandro could remember asking him for details of his mother until eventually he'd given up. They had retreated into their own worlds and it was a relationship that worked for both of them. There was no room for any sudden curiosity about a scrapbook his father had kept over the years.

'You're quite the Good Samaritan, aren't you?' he murmured softly.

This was where he felt comfortable. He could relax when he was playing a game of seduction and he was certainly relaxed when he noticed the shell-pink colour that rose to her cheeks at his change of tone.

He reached out and delicately brushed a tendril of hair from her face and then he left his finger there, tracing her soft cheek until he was trailing it along her mouth.

This was where he was supposed to be.

Not thinking crazy thoughts that weren't going to get anyone anywhere...

But right here, touching her and putting an end to the will-they, won't-they game. Those sorts of games were tiresome. Reduced to its barest bones, the chemistry between them was as powerful as a live current and there was no way that a three-act tragedy about why she shouldn't sleep with him should get in the way.

Caught in a balancing act of wondering what she should or shouldn't do, Laura allowed her body to sink into that feathery touch. Her mouth trembled and she half closed her eyes, released a small sigh. She wasn't even aware of raising her hands so that she could curl her fingers into the lapels of his coat, or of reaching up on her toes, her whole body leaning towards him and demanding more than just the touch of his finger on her skin.

Her mind went blank when she felt the coolness of his mouth hit hers. She couldn't get enough. She returned the kiss urgently, fiercely seeking out his tongue. Her breasts were pushed against the rock-hard wall of his chest and she nearly collapsed when he shifted his big hands underneath her jumper and cradled them.

Her nipples itched and strained against her bra. She wanted to reach behind and rip it off because the need to have him touch her without the barrier of itchy, starchy fabric was overwhelming.

Somehow he had managed to manoeuvre her against the wall without breaking the contact of their kiss.

Nothing, but nothing, had ever felt like this before. So

this was what it felt like to be submerged in a tidal wave of passion.

He cupped her bottom, shifted her so that she could feel the hot steel of his erection, and she squirmed against it.

'I don't care,' she broke away to whisper, and he looked at her. 'I'm not going to be careful. I want you. You were right. I want you so badly…'

Alessandro was so turned on that he feared the unthinkable might happen, especially as the chances of them ending up in a bed somewhere were remote, not while Edith was asleep upstairs.

When he took her, he wanted to do it slowly, without having to listen out just in case her grandmother came flying out of a bedroom somewhere.

It shouldn't matter but somehow it did. For once, he wasn't operating in his usual vacuum, where he had no one to whom he had to refer and no one whose opinion mattered.

'We can't…here…' He was breathing heavily and his hands were shaking ever so slightly as he set her apart from him. 'Trust me, I would sling you over my shoulder and take those stairs two at a time to the nearest bed, but…'

'But Gran's upstairs. I know.' She straightened her jumper and did something with her hair.

'Dream of me tonight,' he said roughly. 'When we make love, I want to take my time.' He sifted his fingers through her hair, marvelling at its sexy, silky length. 'Trust me, Laura, it'll be worth the wait…'

CHAPTER SEVEN

FROM ALWAYS MAINTAINING a polite distance, Alessandro found, over the next week or so, that his father now seemed to be around constantly.

The sale of the house, as he had confidently predicted, was all progressing nicely. It just went to show that anyone could be bought, because the Saunders children, having initially made noises about their sentimental attachment to the place, jettisoned all that the second there was a concrete and very inflated offer on the table. In fact, they couldn't hurry things on fast enough.

Builders were on standby, ready to begin work on renovations, and his father wanted a say on every single detail of those renovations.

'Not being shoved out of my own house to find myself in a dump!' he had bellowed the evening before as they had sat at the kitchen table, poring over plans.

'I'll get Edith along to back you up when you say that you're being *shoved out*, shall I?' Alessandro had countered. 'I'm thinking she might have a different take on the matter.'

Frankly, he was finding it almost impossible to concentrate on anything, never mind where a greenhouse was going to go, because Roberto Falcone was going nowhere unless there was a greenhouse of a specific size that could house specific plants, flowers and vegetables. Alessandro was making the occasional trip back down to the city, but for the most part he was working from his makeshift office, and for the first time in his life focus was proving a problem.

Laura had somehow eroded his perfectly ordered life and he had quickly worked out that that was because they still hadn't slept together. He saw a lot of her…every evening she came to the house, where they would go through rooms, working out what could go, what could stay and what needed to be packed by them. And every evening, the brush of his fingers against hers as he reached for something, the slightest physical contact, sent his blood pressure soaring. It was a form of protracted foreplay that was driving him crazy. There were a thousand times when he would have taken her in whatever part of whatever room they'd happened to be in, but for his everpresent father.

Never had it taken him so long to get nowhere with any woman. And the longer it took, the more he wanted her. He couldn't get her out of his head. Returning to London full-time and shifting the overseeing of this project to any one of the many, many capable people he could call upon was out of the question.

Now, at a little after six, he pushed himself away from his desk, stretched and sauntered to the window to stare out at a pitch-black nightscape.

There would be no Laura this evening. Parents meeting at the school, apparently. He couldn't remember his father ever being interested in something as mundane as attending a parents' meeting. He had always been abroad, away on business. A suitable replacement had always been sent, usually a nanny.

Realising that it would be a pointless exercise to continue trying to work, he began sorting through the lower reaches of the bookcase that stood against the wall. He'd never noticed them before but since every nook and cranny in the house seemed to contain something, he felt he wouldn't be disappointed.

Alessandro heard the bustle of his father in the kitchen before he entered. The door was ajar and he could make him out, yet again neatly attired in formal clothes, as though the Queen might take it into her head to pay him an unexpected visit for which he had to be ready. They had dumped the formal dining room a while back for the informality of the kitchen. At least in a smaller arena the silences weren't quite so resounding.

He inhaled deeply and glanced down at the wad of envelopes in his hand. They were sepia with age.

'Found one or two things,' he said, walking in, knowing that this was something that had to be confronted. He watched as his father turned around and then he strolled towards the kitchen table and dumped the envelopes down. 'Why didn't you tell me?'

'Tell you what?' Roberto adjusted his tie and cast a baleful look at his son.

'You know what. Why didn't you tell me about my past?'

An hour and a half later, Alessandro was on his way to see Laura. For once, he had no desire to be on his own. He and his father could have continued talking into the night but they were too accustomed to their silences for that. They had stopped talking when both had felt that everything that had been said needed to be digested.

He killed the engine of his car and sat in the darkness for a few seconds, before swinging out and heading to the front door. He half expected Edith to get it but she didn't. Seeing him there, Laura's eyes opened wide, then she stepped aside so that he could brush past her.

'I've only just got back from the parents' meeting,' she said, eyeing him nervously as he prowled into the sitting room and, once there, remained standing by the window, having divested himself of his coat.

'Where's your grandmother?'

'What are you doing here? She's having dinner with friends in the village…why?' Her heart fluttered and she wanted to ask him if he just couldn't stand it any longer, if he had had to come because days of being in the same space, clearing out Roberto's stuff while he'd watched like a relentless chaperone, had been as difficult for him as it had been for her.

Alessandro saw the blaze of unbidden desire in her eyes and smiled slowly. 'Fortuitous.' He put down his coat and walked towards her. 'Been thinking of me?'

'I've seen quite a bit of you recently so why would I…?' Laura went bright red. Yes, she had made her mind up that this was what she was going to do. She wasn't going to fight lust. There were so many reasons for just giving in but there was a limit to what she was ever going to admit. She certainly wasn't going to admit that she had been thinking of him…something about that sentiment would have made her feel uneasy, although she didn't know why because he had said it lightly, jokingly.

'Do you know, I have never…' he was right up close to her now and he hooked his fingers into the waistband of her jogging bottoms and began slowly tugging them down '…spent so long…' he propelled her backwards, in small steps, until she had her back to the wall '…in the company of a woman I've wanted…' the jogging bottoms were halfway down her legs, but instead of removing her panties he slipped his finger under the silky fabric, unerringly finding the wet slit between her thighs '...and been forced to practise such self-restraint...'

He began stroking her, rubbing her clitoris, losing himself in the sensation, letting it flood his mind and overwhelm the raging confusion of his thoughts.

This was exactly what he needed.

Right here. Right now. His chaotic mind was silenced. He felt her wetness and his mind went completely blank, allowing pure sensation to flood through.

'I have wanted this for so long...' he muttered, as she squirmed against his exploring finger, barely capable of breathing. 'I don't want to make love to you here, standing by the front door, with you pushed up against the wall...'

'We can go up to my bedroom...'

'And I don't want your grandmother walking in on us...'

'She won't. She's having dinner with friends and then they're going to the town hall fifteen miles away to hear a lecture on orchids. There'll be a lot of questions...'

'Where's your bedroom?' He drew back, his dark eyes giving her the opportunity to back off, but he didn't know what he would do if she did. He was so tightly wound that he could scarcely think straight.

Laura trembled, linked her fingers through his, and they took the stairs quietly and quickly up to her room.

He had caught her unawares. She hadn't had time to anticipate or for her nerves to build, but her heart was beating fast and when they reached her bedroom she paused as the enormity of what she was about to do sank in.

Was this *her*? *Really*? What had happened to the dream of finding Mr Right? What had happened to her resolution never to have any sort of relationship with any guy who wasn't going to be there for her as a life partner?

When she had made that resolution, she hadn't known about Alessandro, she thought ruefully. She hadn't yet discovered that there would be someone out there capable of driving all those careful plans out of her head. It just hadn't seemed possible at the time, not when she had felt bitter and wounded.

When it came to women, Alessandro Falcone was a taker. Those lazy, dark eyes saw, desired, conquered and then, shortly after, when his appetite had been sated, he dismissed.

He had no sense of anything aside from himself. He had no sense of family, no sense of wanting to start a family of his own, no belief in love, no ability to give commitment. He represented everything she abhorred and yet...

Here I am now...

She didn't switch on the overhead light. Instead, she turned on her bedside lamp, which sent a dull, mellow glow through the room.

'You seem to have a thing for dogs...' For a few seconds Alessandro took time out to glance at the room, which was small and cosy. There was a rocking chair by the window in which sat an assortment of stuffed dogs.

'I should have got rid of them a long time ago.' Laura laughed a little self-consciously. 'I always wanted a dog but Gran put her foot down at that and decided that stuffed dogs would do the trick. I've never been able to bring myself to dump them. They're too much a part of my past.'

Alessandro strolled towards her. 'We have something in common. I wanted a dog as well but, of course, in a boarding school pets were not permitted. I don't want to talk. I want to touch. Take off all those clothes. Let me see you naked.'

After the briefest of hesitations, during which some small voice urged caution, she began doing as he asked. She ignored the small voice. This was her choice, to live in the present, to enjoy this man with no strings attached.

If there were no strings attached, she wouldn't be disappointed. She knew what she was getting into and she was going into it with her eyes wide open.

And it was now or never. Her grandmother wouldn't be back for at least a couple of hours. There was no opportunity to do anything at the big house as Roberto was always around. He seemed to think that unless he was supervising things, valuable possessions would end up in the bin.

This was a golden opportunity and then she knew that he would walk away. They would both leave this behind but right now her want and her need poured through her like a deadly virus and the only way she could clear her system of it was to do what she was going to do, to sleep with this beautiful, arrogant, clever and utterly inappropriate man.

The jumper was on the floor and she unclasped her bra. She could feel his eyes on her and it was a little thrilling, if she was honest. The cool air hit her hot, naked breasts like soothing balm. The sort of women he dated didn't have breasts and she feverishly wondered what he thought of hers. Bigger than he had expected? Not neat and small enough?

Her breath was coming and going in painful gasps as he moved towards her and she fell into his arms, enjoying the way his jumper eased some of the pain of her sensitive nipples. She rubbed herself against him and he lifted her ear and whispered,

'You have the most amazing breasts...'

'They're far too big.'

'Amazing breasts and even more amazing nipples.'

'Too big as well.'

'That's not possible.' He propelled her gently towards the bed, which was unfortunately not king-sized, and Laura fell back onto the pillows with a heated sigh.

In the semi-darkness of the bedroom, Alessandro took a few seconds to just look at her. His erection was a shaft of steel, almost painful, but he had to regain some of his self-control or lose it completely.

Her arms were folded behind her head so that her breasts were pushed up, offering themselves to him like ripe, succulent fruit. She had removed her jogging bottoms but her panties were still on and he knew that if he felt them, they would be soaked through.

He got rid of his jumper and the T-shirt underneath. His hand loose on the button of his trousers, he took a few deep breaths and then pulled down the zipper, very slowly, taking his time. He didn't want to rush this but, God, he was close to coming just looking at her and at the drowsy smile tugging the corners of her mouth as she watched him.

'Enjoying the striptease?' he murmured roughly, and her smile broadened. She wriggled a little on the bed, parted her legs, and Alessandro emitted a low, unsteady groan.

'I've never been treated to one before,' she told him truthfully.

She was so turned on that she could barely get the words out. Even in the dim light she could see the proud bulge of his erection and she cupped her mound, then slid her hand under the panties because she was hurting down there, aching to be touched.

Alessandro stepped out of his trousers, then the boxers, retrieving a condom from his wallet, although he wasn't even conscious of doing so.

He flicked it onto the bedside table and remained standing next to the bed, completely naked.

He was bigger than big, Laura thought. Big all over. A broad-shouldered, powerfully built man and his erection was beyond impressive. She propped herself up on one hand and took him into her mouth, feeling him shudder with a kick of heady satisfaction.

He arched his back and his hand pressed to the back of her head, urging her to suck him, to taste him.

She licked and teased and played with him and his deep groans were impossibly sexy.

When he could take it no more he tugged himself free of her eager mouth and remained perfectly still, controlling his breathing with difficulty.

Finally, he looked down at her. 'I have never wanted any woman the way I want you now.'

Laura wasn't going to analyse that. She fell back onto the pillows, legs parted, and moaned softly when he joined her.

He kissed her slowly, taking his time, his tongue exploring her mouth, then he moved to trail kisses along her jawline. She arched up and then sighed, eyes fluttering shut as he took one nipple into his mouth and began suckling on it, lazy and thorough.

She was drowning in sensation and it was nothing like anything she had felt before.

This must be what it felt like to lose control utterly and completely, knowing that what you were enjoying was a one-off experience that had to be appreciated to the absolute utmost because it wasn't going anywhere and would probably not be repeated.

She was filled with a feeling of liberation. When he slipped his hand underneath her panties, she spread her legs a little wider and gasped as he began stroking her clitoris.

He rubbed his finger insistently over the throbbing nub until she was pleading with him to stop. She didn't want to come like this…

Alessandro straddled her. Opening her eyes to gaze at

him, Laura didn't think that she had ever seen anyone quite so beautiful and she felt that she probably never would again.

She held him in her hands but he gently disengaged her with a smile.

'This isn't just about my satisfaction,' he murmured huskily. 'This is about you as well…' He leaned down to lick her stomach, which was salty with perspiration, then he moved lower until his mouth was on her panties, and without removing them he teased her until she squirmed, until she could barely stand the intense excitement building inside her, an explosion that was on the brink of detonating.

Only then did he ever so slowly pull down her underwear, where it joined the heap of clothes on the floor.

He liked the way she wasn't all skin and bone. The soft roundness of her hips was an exquisite turn-on. Her breasts were abundant, succulent, and he could have stayed buried in them for far, far longer.

He breathed in the musky, honeyed scent between her legs and then gently slid his tongue into her, finding her clitoris once more, but this time the delicate thrust of his moist tongue was a mind-blowing experience for her. She instinctively reached down, curling her fingers into his dark hair, raising her legs slightly so that he could sink his tongue deeper into her.

She knew that she was groaning but the sounds she was making seemed to be coming from someone else, far away.

He teased her until she was going mad with wanting him, until the only satisfaction she needed was to have him in her, and in between the groans she knew that she was pleading with him to stop, to come inside her, that she *needed* him…*right now*…

'Demanding hussy.' Alessandro reached for the condom

and applied it with shaky fingers, resenting that brief interruption, that momentary parting of their bodies.

But he needed to come inside her, too, as much as she needed it.

Foreplay was all well and good but the tipping point had come far too close and far too often for his liking.

He thrust long and deep into her, loving her tight wetness and the way her legs slid up and around his waist so that he could reach and cup her buttocks in his big hands.

He would have liked to have exercised control. And he did, but he was driven to move faster, harder, and he knew that she had come when he felt her body stiffen and heard the rhythm of her breathing faster and faster, more and more breathless, until she was crying out and gasping at the same time.

Only then, and thankfully not a second too soon, did he allow himself the ultimate release. He reared back and reached an unbelievable orgasm on one deep thrust.

Caught in the grip of the physical, he had managed to set aside the ground-shaking conversation he had had with his father. Now, as he lay down next to her and felt the curve of her rounded body lean against him, Alessandro frowned, reliving that conversation.

The room felt too small and he swung his legs over the side of the bed and walked restlessly towards the window.

Laura felt a chill run through her and she sat up, pulling the quilt over her and clutching it under her breasts.

She had enjoyed her no-strings-attached experience and this was what the comedown felt like. Horrible. They had made love and now he couldn't even stand the thought of staying next to her in the bed for five seconds.

Hit-and-run was the expression that sprang to mind, but there was no way she was going to start raising objections or asking for more than he was prepared to give.

She had no idea what to say in a situation like this. She could feel a hollow emptiness clawing at her throat and she shot him a brave smile.

Alessandro noted that brave smile and raked his fingers through his hair. He'd sated his physical needs and he knew he should walk away. He also knew that he wasn't going to do that. Not yet. He'd had her and he wanted more.

He also needed…for the first time in his life after sex… to do more than glance at his watch and bring proceedings to an end.

'Has my father ever confided in you?' he asked abruptly, and she was so startled at his question that she stared at him in round-eyed silence. 'And please don't try lying to me.'

'Alessandro, I have no idea what you're talking about.'

'You and he seem to enjoy a close relationship and then throw your grandmother into the mix and we have a little circle of who knows what kind of touchy-feely confidence-sharing…' He remained by the window, propped against the ledge, arms folded, still completely and gloriously naked.

'Are you going to start accusing me of being a gold-digger all over again?' she asked tersely. 'Are you going to try insinuating that my grandmother and I are involved in some kind of seedy plot to take your father for everything he's got?' She felt tears sting the backs of her eyes. It was one thing to have a one-night stand with someone who was allergic to relationships, but it was something else to have a one-night stand and then be shoved into the firing line.

'I thought you'd got past all of that.'

Alessandro shook his head and pushed himself away from the window ledge to begin scooping up his clothes, his movements oddly lacking their usual grace.

'You found a scrapbook,' he said roughly. Jeans on, shirt

on, though with the buttons undone, he moved to stand by the bed, looking down at her with brooding intensity.

'Oh, yes. That. Alessandro, I don't know what you're talking about and you're making me nervous, standing there and glowering down at me.'

'What else might you have found that you failed to deliver to me?'

'*Deliver to you?* Is that what you think I should be doing? Sorting through your father's stuff and then handing over anything I think you might want to see? Even if it would be up to Roberto to do the handing over himself? Do you think I should be using this opportunity to *spy* on your father? See if he's been investing in anything dodgy? Or maybe sending money abroad because he's been scammed by some crooks somewhere? Or maybe he's just been hiding something you think you should know about! Because you should know *everything*, shouldn't you?'

'Should I?' He walked away and sat at the little chair by her dressing table, dwarfing it with his big, muscular frame. 'Well, it would appear not. I mean, I never knew, for starters, that my mother died giving birth to me.'

Laura gasped and sat forward. *'What?'*

'My father didn't share that with you?' He raked his fingers through his hair. He hadn't meant to say anything. He had needed to lose himself in her, had thought that sex would have been enough to still the turmoil in his head. Obviously not.

'No. He didn't. I...I don't understand. How is it that you're only now finding out about...about your mother?' She reached down to the side of the bed and yanked at her jumper, sticking it on and then wriggling into her underwear.

She couldn't remain lying down while he sat there...

She realised now how utterly self-controlled he was

now that that self-control had slipped. His expression was bleak and she just needed to hold him, touch him, but not in a sexual manner. She felt driven *to be there for him*, although that need barely registered as conscious thought.

There was a little rocking chair by the window, another legacy from her childhood, and she dragged it over so that she could sit right next to him. He didn't object when she laced her fingers through his.

'What else...?'

'What other revelations were aired? Now, let's see. Oh, yes, I had a sister. She died when she was twelve. Fell from a tree, of all things.'

'Alessandro...'

'That's when they decided that having another child might be a good idea. Or rather, reading between the lines, my mother thought it... Do you know something? I have no idea why I'm telling you this.'

'Because everyone needs to vent now and again.'

'I feel you might be confusing me with a loser.'

'Are you upset with him? Angry?' She ignored his dry dismissal of having feelings, of being vulnerable. She would have done anything to wipe the haunted expression from his face because it just didn't belong there.

'Both.' Alessandro shot her a crooked smile. Upset. Angry. Yes, he was both those things but in time those feelings would disappear and he knew that he would be grateful for the conversation he and his father had had, the revelations that had been made.

He was finally understanding why his father had been the remote figure in his life, how his grief over the loss of his much younger wife had somehow transferred into distance from the son he had held responsible.

'I was an old fool,' Roberto had growled, as uncomfortable with sharing his feelings as his son was, 'but the longer time went by, the more impossible it became to remedy the damage, and in the end there was just the silence between us. Should have opened up, explained everything. Got pictures of your mother. Loved that woman more than anything in the world. Would have died for her. When you're ready to forgive the old fool, you're welcome to see the pictures.'

'You know,' Laura said thoughtfully, 'he never talked about where he lived before he came here. There was always a part of himself that he kept hidden away from all of us.' Her fingers were still linked through his. This felt like a moment in time she wanted to bottle and keep for ever and it confused her because what they had meant nothing. They were like two ships passing in the night. They didn't have any sort of *relationship*. So why did she feel as though her heart was breaking when she imagined his life, growing up, when she saw the bleakness in his eyes? Why did she want to make it *all better*?

Alessandro shrugged. She could feel him begin to withdraw from her and she panicked at the thought that he might resent the fact that he had confided, that she had seen him with his guard down, as vulnerable as he was ever likely to be. He was a proud man, the lion accustomed to standing alone.

Now she knew why and she felt for him.

'Did you...come here...to make love to me...because...?'

Alessandro flushed darkly. 'I wanted you,' he said gruffly. 'I don't analyse things before that. And I should go now, before your grandmother returns home and catches me in a compromising situation with her granddaughter.' He began buttoning up his shirt but he didn't take his eyes from her.

He'd never confided in anyone before but he wasn't sorry he'd done so.

'I think,' he drawled, back to his usual self, 'that the

next time we should consider somewhere with a slightly less restricted bed.'

Her heart soared. *So there was going to be a next time...*

'When my grandmother bought me this bed...' she stuck on her jogging bottoms, feeling lighter now because he wasn't going to waltz off into the sunset and leave her behind just yet '...I was twelve. I never imagined I'd need a bigger one because I would one day find myself here with a guy...'

They walked back down the stairs but before they reached the door she rested her small hand on his arm.

'Are you going to be all right?'

Alessandro looked down into her clear, concerned, green eyes and smiled lazily.

'Are you feeling sorry for me?'

She immediately removed her hand. 'I'm sorry for both of you,' she answered honestly. 'For all the time you've lost.'

'I'll go,' Alessandro said, in that same tone of voice that told her that the confidences were over and would not be returning, 'before you decide that you need to give me a hug. I've never been one who saw the point of hugs when it came to women. So many more exciting things to do and, unfortunately for us, not quite enough time at the moment.'

But something about the sincere sympathy in her open, honest, clear-eyed gaze got to him.

She hadn't been gushy in her sympathy. She hadn't tried to plead with him to stay so that she could try to take advantage of his once-in-a-lifetime lapse in self-control. She hadn't plied him with concerned questions and then offered some repeat sex to take the pain away or any such nonsense.

But, then, she was in a league of her own. She wasn't part of his London life, wasn't dating him, wasn't looking for anything more than what they had, which was a brief and highly enjoyable fling, the result of circumstances more than anything else. She knew his father. In many ways their lives were entwined, which was certainly a situation he had never catered for.

And she was a fantastic lover.

As he drove away, he felt himself harden at the memory of their lovemaking. She was responsive, eager, not trying to impress him with gymnastic skill and not making noises about meeting up soon for an encore.

In receipt of his father's confidences, she had been just what he had needed.

And he knew that he wanted more of her.

His father was asleep by the time he got home. Tomorrow they would talk again. Laura had been right when she had said that she felt sorry for both of them and the time they had wasted, the years that had raced by during which he had been ignorant of the jigsaw-puzzle pieces of his past.

He had assumed that his father had been as remote with his wife as he had been with his son. He had been wrong. His father had been giddy with love and when he had lost her he had lost the will to carry on. Certainly, he had lost all desire to bond with the son who was a painful reminder of the woman he had loved and lost. He had buried himself in his work to the exclusion of everything else, using it as a crutch to get him through the loneliness.

For once Alessandro went to bed without first checking his emails, making sure that everything that should be happening in his company was happening.

His father was already up and about by the time he hit the kitchen the next morning, and there were two black leather boxes on his side of the table.

'More where those came from,' Roberto said gruffly. 'And don't just stand there staring at them, my boy! Open them up! Should have given them to you a long time ago.'

Alessandro looked at his father, who was busying himself with the kettle and a mug, fetching stuff from one of the kitchen cupboards. 'Well…' Roberto turned around, studiously keeping his eyes averted, and waved an impatient hand '…what are you waiting for? Be dead by the time you make your mind up! Want you to get to know your mother. Should have done it a long time ago. Would have, but…'

'Time runs away,' Alessandro finished succinctly. 'Don't worry. I intend to look at all those photos.'

'Forgive me, boy?'

Alessandro had never thought he would be having this conversation with his father or hearing those words, and something deep in the core of him shifted. 'Depends…' he drawled.

'On what, eh?'

'On how cooperative you are about moving into the cottage before the greenhouse has been built to your absolute specifications…because that's proving a little trickier than you'd expect…'

Roberto relaxed, shot him a gruff smile. 'I'm an old man. Not sure I can make compromises with my tomatoes and orchids. I'll give it my best shot, though.'

CHAPTER EIGHT

LAURA DIDN'T KNOW what to expect when she came to the house the following morning.

A bitter wind had got up and light flurries of snow speckled a yellow-grey sky. Winter had been strangely polite for the past few weeks but now she could feel it getting ready to make up for lost ground. It was always the way in this part of the world. No civilised, rainy, fairly temperate winters but brutal, freezing-cold ones punctuated by blizzards and dense snowfalls.

She had left her grandmother sorting out the log pile with the radio on full blast and she was relieved that she was on her own. She needed time to get her thoughts in order.

The night before had shaken her. She hadn't expected Alessandro to show up at the house. The way they had spent so much time circling around one another…sharing the odd thrilling touch when Roberto's attention had happened to be elsewhere… It had turned into an almost surreal situation. The reality of their one kiss had become imbued with a dreamlike quality and sometimes she had questioned whether it had really happened or not.

She had wondered if they would ever make love. Or was this just a game they would play, almost getting there but not quite, until the time came when he disappeared over the horizon, never to be seen again or else to be seen only in passing?

She had known that if he disappeared over that horizon, then that would be it. He would fall back into his London life and she would become an almost-there non-experience that he would look back upon with…

She didn't know. Mild regret? Relief? Amusement?

The longer they had circled one another, sharing fleeting glances, the more she felt that they would never make love, even though it was what she had wanted more than anything else.

So when he had turned up unannounced, she had been thrilled, apprehensive, seized with soaring excitement.

And if she'd had any doubts about her decision, they had evaporated the second he had touched her. Sooner. The second she had answered the door to him.

Driving through the snow flurries, she was oblivious to the gathering white around her because she was so immersed in her thoughts.

She had thought he had come to her because he hadn't been able to bear the edge-of-the-cliff suspense that had developed between them, the agonising feeling of wanting something that was just beyond reach. She had thought that he had reached the end of his tether and had found the situation as frustrating as she had.

Yes, he had wanted her but he had come to her because he had wanted physical release and she couldn't help but feel that any willing body might have done at a pinch. He had been dealt a bolt from the blue, had been given an overload of information, and the only way he had been able to process that had been through making love. He was an intensely physical man and it would have made complete sense to him to subdue whatever upset he had been feeling by sleeping with a woman, by losing himself in the act of sex.

It was painful for her to accept that if she hadn't been there, he might have just had one of his many devoted fans flown up to sate his passing need.

And yet he had said that he still wanted her.

Laura knew that she should have killed that at source but she had cravenly succumbed to the pleasurable notion that their weird, fragile relationship might carry on for a little longer.

Now, as she neared the big house, she wondered whether that hadn't just been pie in the sky, something he had said on the spur of the moment because he hadn't been himself. People said all sorts of things when they weren't themselves. He had let his guard slip with her and she knew instinctively that he hadn't planned on that happening. He was a guy who liked complete and absolute control. His formidable control had been dealt a near lethal blow and he had, against all his better judgement, opened up to her. Partially. Enough for her to think that the best thing she could do now would be to pretend that everything was fine, that nothing had changed.

She wasn't going to make noises about wanting him. She wasn't going to let him think that he had to worry about her trying to manoeuvre him into a cubbyhole somewhere because he had made a mistake and said stuff he hadn't meant to say.

She certainly wasn't going to try to encourage him to open up to her, to really express what he felt about what he had been told by his father, the secrets that had been revealed, even though that was something she wanted more than anything.

And that, she thought, pulling to a stop in the courtyard, scared her.

She stared out at the falling snow and frowned. Of course she would be empathetic to anyone whose life had been blighted in the way Alessandro's had been, but what she felt was more than detached empathy and that frightened her. The emotions running through her felt complicated and involved, and with a sigh of frustration she headed towards the house, knowing that the only way to deal with the situation was to ignore it.

So when she rang the doorbell and Alessandro opened the door, she smiled politely and informed him, in a bouncy voice, that she had come to help, if more help was needed, with some of the packing.

She was wrapped up in several layers but she made sure not to begin removing any of them just in case he told her that her help wouldn't be needed.

'I probably wouldn't have come if I'd realised how fast the snow was falling,' she chirruped, 'but by the time my windscreen wipers were on full blast I was practically turning into your drive...' It was an effort to meet those dark, penetrating eyes. He hadn't shaved and he didn't look as though he had run a comb through his hair, but instead of looking untidy he looked dangerously, heart-stoppingly sexy. She wanted to stare and stare. She felt the pulse beating frantically in her neck and her mouth was dry, so dry that she was finding it difficult to swallow.

He was in a pair of faded, low-slung jeans and an old rugby sweater, with just a pair of loafers on his feet. No socks. He couldn't have looked more casual and yet more sophisticated.

Alessandro stared down at her, frowning because this was just the sort of unenthusiastic greeting he didn't want. Not when he had spent most of the night consumed by her, thoughts of her, her smell, her taste, the feel of her under his hands, under his mouth, under his body. He had wanted, *needed*, to drown out his thoughts in her glorious body and he had, so what was wrong with expecting a little more of the teasing temptress when he wanted a repeat performance? Naturally, it would have been too much to maybe expect her to turn up wearing a fur coat with nothing underneath because that would have been utterly impractical and, besides, it wasn't her style. But she *could* have made some attempt to collar him by the front door and drag him off to the nearest vacant room...

After a night of beyond-fantastic sex, safe in the knowledge that he hadn't yet lost interest, there wasn't a single woman he could think of who wouldn't have been planning just how to hold and maintain his interest. Any woman would have shown up in her sexiest house-clearing clothes, feather duster in hand and a very good idea of what she was going to do with it.

A quick glance was enough to tell him that underneath her layers and layers and yet more layers of clothes Laura was probably fully kitted out in her most sensible underwear. He didn't imagine she even owned a feather duster, and if she had it would have been used strictly for dusting.

So they weren't going to get wrapped up in any sort of happy-ever-after scenario, but nevertheless...

He leaned nonchalantly against the door frame and folded his arms. 'There's always time to back up and leave the way you came,' he said coolly. 'Wouldn't want you to be trapped here by falling snow. Happens in this part of the world. I've been told often enough by my father.'

Laura's eyes skittered away and she felt a lump form at the back of her throat.

'You don't want me here, in other words,' she said flatly.

'Come in.' He stepped aside, allowing her to brush past him. Was she going to pretend that they hadn't made love?

he wondered. The mere thought that she might go down that road staggered him.

'Where's Roberto? I'd love to go and have a chat with him. I haven't seen him properly to talk to for a while.' She glanced beyond his shoulder because it gave her eyes time to take a rest from their compulsive staring.

'He's in his greenhouse, having a quick chat to his plants to make sure they're up for the upheaval of moving.' Roberto? *Roberto?* She shouldn't be *asking* about his father! She should be taking advantage of their brief window of privacy to source the nearest empty room!

Women chased Alessandro. He had never really had any need to try. He had the looks, he had the money and he had that all-important invisible aphrodisiac called *power*. He had always been able to enjoy his position of strength from the top of his ivory tower, safe in the expectation that people would come to him and never, ever the other way around.

He had trained himself to enjoy his formidable independence, had liked the fact that he had never had to adjust any part of his life to accommodate anyone else.

His boarding-school experience, pleasant though it had been, had turned him into someone who needed no one and sought no one's approval. The one thing to be said for an absolute lack of family life was that it gave you strength of character, and as far as Alessandro was concerned, that was more important than anything else.

So it was as frustrating as hell to now find himself on the back foot while she continued to frown and scour the hallway as if he had deliberately hidden his father from her.

'Perhaps I could go see him, take him a cup of tea before we get down to the business of clearing...'

There was nothing she had just said that Alessandro was interested in hearing.

'How is he dealing with…? How are you *both* dealing with everything that's happened? I hope you don't mind but I've told my grandmother some of what you said to me, and it seems that she *did* know bits and pieces…'

Alessandro relaxed. This was more like it. Sympathy… tears glistening in eyes…a trembling hand gently laid on his arm…

Under *any* other circumstances he would have been repelled at having his private life regurgitated for the purposes of speculation. It had to be said, though, that he would never have confided in anyone else and the only reason he had felt the need to confide in Laura was because of her connection to his father. And the fact that she was raising the subject now…well, he wasn't going to shoot her down in flames, even though he wasn't about to oblige her by launching into some long, tear-jerking, over-sentimental nonsense. In fact…

'He's fine. We're both fine. It's been…an eye-opener, hearing what my father has had to say.' He jerked his head in the direction of the kitchen. 'I always wondered why the kitchen was so full of old furniture. It seems that when my father moved from the cottage where he and my mother lived, the kitchen furniture, along with the oven, were the only reminders he took of the life he left behind.' He frowned, not sure whether he had intended saying so much.

'I always wondered where he had lived before and how it was he never, ever spoke about it…'

'Cup of coffee?'

'Huh?'

'I'll make you a cup of coffee before we kick-start the day.'

'Right. Sure.' Message received loud and clear. He wasn't going to take her into his confidence again. Why should he? She was a fling and flings didn't qualify for that kind of depth. 'Maybe I could pop out…see your dad…'

'He'll be in shortly,' Alessandro said irritably, spinning on his heel and making for the kitchen. 'You don't need to fuss around him like a mother hen, Laura. When he goes to his greenhouse it's because he needs downtime on his own, not because he wants a queue of people lining up to bring him cups of tea and bracing chats.'

'You're so sarcastic,' she muttered, following him and divesting herself of some of her clothes on the way. By the time she made it to the kitchen door she was down to her fleece. How was it that her *casual* managed to look so charity shop? The jeans were okay but it was really cold out and she had worn her thermal knee-high socks, pulled up over the skinny jeans, both of which were tucked into her fur-lined boots. She knew she looked a sight. She had bunched her hair up into a woolly hat and now it was released into all its crazy glory.

Was he looking at her and wondering how on earth he had been idiotic enough to have ever found her attractive?

He'd made absolutely no mention of renewing any kind of relationship and that, she told herself, was probably for the best.

So why did she feel sick and hollow inside?

He had his back to her as he made them both a cup of coffee and when he turned around she made sure to school her features into the polite smile of someone whose thoughts were far removed from sex.

'Come again?' Alessandro sauntered towards her. Her fleece was an unappealing shade of green but the jeans were nicely tight and even the strange socks halfway up her calves did nothing to detract from the bolt of pure lust that ripped through him.

In his head, he had a perfectly good image of what she

looked like underneath the layers. He could recreate the taste of her and the feel of her with no trouble at all.

'Nothing,' she muttered, taking the mug from him and sidling across to the table, where she sat, blowing on the hot coffee and keeping her eyes pointedly averted.

'Tell me what game we're playing,' Alessandro drawled, moving to perch on the table right next to where she was sitting so that she was forced to look up at him.

'Game?' Laura parroted feebly.

'Because if it's the game of playing hard to get, you can scrap it before it begins.'

'I have no idea what you're talking about!'

'I'm talking about the polite semi-stranger act you're busy trying to perfect.'

'I'm not about to start chasing you, Alessandro.' Laura abandoned the tactic of pretending to misunderstand what he was saying. 'And I'm not playing hard to get. I don't play games!' She glared at him.

'So are we going to both make-believe that last night didn't happen? Shall we enter a conspiracy of silence?'

'I know what you're like and I'm not going to be one of those women who gets clingy in the aftermath of sex.'

'What am I like?'

'You run away from forming relationships faster than a speeding bullet,' she told him bluntly. 'I bet the second a woman starts making plans, you start wondering where the nearest exit is.'

Alessandro laughed, his dark eyes roving over her flushed face appreciatively. 'I like your sense of humour,' he murmured in a voice that was the equivalent of oozing, liquid chocolate, the sort of voice that made her knees feel like jelly and turned her brains into instant mush.

'And I happen to be very good at forming relationships, although, admittedly, they're not of the lasting kind. But that's not relevant with us, is it? You know the measure of me, and after your mistake with a married man you're hardly on the lookout for someone who's not talking long-term. Did you...?' A sudden thought flashed through his head, leaving a sour taste in its wake. 'Did you love the guy?'

'Colin?' She was disconcerted by the question because she didn't think that Alessandro was the sort of man prone to showing much interest in what women had to say about their past relationships. In keeping with someone who planned nothing in advance, because who knew when someone better looking might come along and steal the limelight, she took him for a guy who lived totally for the present. At least in the arena of relationships.

'I thought I did,' she confessed, when the silence threatened to become uncomfortable. 'But I was just swept away by someone cute who knew how to play me. I think I fell in love with the feeling of being in love.' And, in fact, she hardly thought about him and now, sitting here, she could barely remember what he had looked like. 'I suppose you're going to tell me that that's the problem with love. It doesn't exist so it's best to avoid it altogether and just hop in the sack with people you fancy.'

Alessandro smiled slowly and watched as hectic colour invaded her cheeks.

'Would you follow my advice if I told you that?'

'You might not believe in love, but I do.'

'Yet you hopped in the sack with me.'

'You don't have to look so smug about it.'

'I like the thought of you just not being able to help yourself...' He calmly set his mug down on the table and traced the contour of her jaw with a finger.

'That's so arrogant,' Laura told him unevenly.

'I know. I'm arrogant. I want to kiss you and I'm arrogant enough to think that you'd probably like to kiss me back. Am I right? Or are you going to stand up and slap me across my face?'

'Has anyone ever done that?'

'No.' He was smiling at her in a way that made her whole body feel as though it had been plugged into a light socket.

'I don't know why I'm attracted to you,' she said with devastating honesty.

'That's a line of introspection you shouldn't bother wasting time with. There's no mileage in it. Go with the flow.' He tugged her hair gently and she stood up on shaky legs.

She wasn't just *attracted* to him, she thought, she was mesmerised by him. Was it because he was so out of her league? Or because the circumstances that had brought them together were so surreal? Or was he just so sinfully, unfairly good-looking that he just went around mesmerising women?

She linked her arms loosely around his neck and stepped between his legs. His body heat flooded her and she hiccuped a sigh of guilty pleasure.

They kissed slowly, taking their time. She pulled away briefly and glanced over her shoulder.

'What if your father walks in?'

'He won't.'

'How do you know?'

'I know his habits. He heads out to his greenhouse and stays there for a couple of hours. I only just ventured inside the place a few days ago and found that he's set it up like a room. The only thing it lacks is a bed. He's got a chair there, a table with books. It's life in a jungle without having to pay the airfare...'

Laura giggled. She didn't want to talk about Roberto.

She wanted to feel his lips on hers again and she moved closer, rubbing herself against his chest and kissing him as slowly as he had kissed her. His tongue inside her mouth was driving her half-crazy because she could recall what it had felt like to have it on her breasts, teasing her nipples and then sliding into her, flicking against her clitoris until she had been so close to coming she could have screamed.

She wished she hadn't covered up so well that for him to slide his hand onto her breast would have been a mission. She wished she hadn't worn a bra in the expectation that their episode of lovemaking was something he might have wanted to put behind him. She wanted her whole body to be accessible. She didn't want to be confined in tight jeans. She wanted baggy, loose-fitting jogging bottoms so that she could have parted her legs and his fingers would have easily found her wetness and eased the ache down there.

But in the absence of suitable clothing she kissed him, not even bothering to come up for air because she didn't want to break the physical contact.

Alessandro had never tasted anything so sweet. He absently thought that she had a unique smell, light, clean, radiating the coldness from outside. It filled his nostrils and was as powerful on his senses as a drug.

Her breasts, pushing against his chest, were soft, abundant, begging to be touched. If they'd had guaranteed privacy, he wouldn't have hesitated to rip off her clothes, because he ached to feel her naked skin against his.

She had a body a man could get lost in and the beauty of it was that she wasn't even aware of her powerful sex appeal. The catwalk models he had always dated knew the power of their physical appeal and utilised it. No one was ever allowed to bypass them or to forget that they were stunning. They maximised their assets.

Laura Reid downplayed hers. She did her utmost to

blend into the background. She hid her bountiful breasts and camouflaged the lush sexiness of her hips and legs.

He curved his hand over her bottom and massaged its fullness, then he swept the same hand between her legs and pressed hard so that his knuckles were kneading her, seeking to find that throbbing little bud underneath the thick denim.

It took them both a couple of seconds before they recognised the sharp rap of a walking stick on the floor, and as if one sharp rap wasn't enough Roberto kept on rapping until they snapped apart and turned to look at him.

Laura felt the hot burn of embarrassment flood her. She was twelve years old again and her grandmother was ticking her off because she had sneaked downstairs to snitch a bar of chocolate in the middle of the night. She ran her trembling fingers through her hair but she couldn't say anything because her vocal cords seemed to have seized up.

Roberto looked absolutely furious.

'This will never do!' His attention was not on her. It was on Alessandro, who, likewise, was temporarily lost for words as his father angrily tapped his way into the kitchen and stood in front of them like a judge about to sentence a couple of criminals.

'What are you talking about?'

'I know what you're like with the women, my boy, and Laura isn't one of those strumpets you take to bed and then discard like a pair of old shoes!'

Alessandro raked his fingers through his hair and glared at his father. 'I don't know what you're talking about.'

'You know exactly what I'm talking about!' He slumped into one of the kitchen chairs and glared balefully at his son. 'I really thought we were beginning to go somewhere with our relationship, son. But straight away I see that I'm never going to understand you.' He fluttered his hand and looked defeated.

'You've got it all wrong,' Alessandro said, and Roberto eyed his son with a glimmer of doubt.

'I come in here and you're making a pass at this young girl!'

'I'm here, Roberto.' Laura finally found her voice and interrupted him before he could resume his attack on Alessandro. 'And it…er…takes two to…er…tango…'

'Nonsense!' Roberto swept aside the interruption while keeping his eyes firmly fixed on his son. 'You don't know Alessandro like I do,' he declared, his voice rising along with his colour.

'Please, Roberto…' She rested her hand anxiously on his shoulder and looked at Alessandro. 'Have you forgotten that you've recently had a stroke?'

'Not likely to when I'm packing up to move because I'm too infirm to stay anywhere that has more than three bedrooms!' He was still staring at Alessandro and he finally said, 'What do you mean when you tell me that *I've got it all wrong*? Fancy explaining yourself, lad?'

'You think you know me,' Alessandro said quietly, defusing the heated atmosphere in a way that Laura could only admire because she had a feeling that giving way like this was just not his style. His physical stillness permeated the room, calming the situation. 'And I admit that my behaviour with women might have seemed a little on the cavalier side…'

Roberto snorted and raised his eyebrows with open cynicism. 'Seemed? *Seemed?*'

'But I realise that Laura isn't—'

'One of those fly-by-night trollops you have one-night stands with? Might be old, son, but I ain't stupid!'

'I never thought you were. What I'm saying…' He had

managed to get himself back in order while, standing to one side, Laura felt as dishevelled as she had fifteen minutes earlier when Roberto had walked in on them.

Alessandro sighed heavily and threw her a very quick look before focusing on his father once more. 'What I'm saying is that this is…different…'

Laura's mouth fell open.

'Laura and I have a very special connection. She's not one of my fly-by-night trollops.' Alessandro thought wryly that some of the catwalk models he'd dated, whose faces adorned high-end fashion magazines, would have been appalled to have been described as *fly-by-night trollops*.

'Special connection?' He humphed and looked between them.

'This is serious,' Alessandro said gravely, and Laura made an effort to rescue her jaw from where it had fully dropped to the floor. Her feet remained nailed down as he moved smoothly to where she was standing and linked his fingers through hers in a gesture that was oddly chaste.

'How serious?' Roberto asked, eyes narrowed, his voice still bearing the traces of lingering scepticism, and Laura, frankly, couldn't blame him. She only hoped that he didn't turn to her for confirmation of what Alessandro had said, because she had no idea where this was going.

Although she did know where it had come from.

He and his father had arrived at a fragile truce after more than two decades of a civilised but frosty relationship. A door, formerly closed, had opened between them. Not fully but enough, and she guessed that Alessandro wasn't about to jeopardise that now. Throw into the mix the fact that Roberto's health was not as robust as it might have been, and she could understand why Alessandro might have found himself in an impossible situation.

'Very serious,' Alessandro said seriously.

'In that case, I'm prepared to give you the benefit of the doubt!' He eyed Laura. 'Edith know about this?'

'No,' Laura said truthfully. As far as she was aware, her grandmother didn't even know that she and Alessandro had anything going on between them but a purely working relationship, but who knew?

'Then if you lovebirds will excuse me…might just go and fill her in.' He waved his hand between them and headed out of the kitchen, leaving in his wake utter and complete silence, which Laura was the first to break.

'What the heck did you just go and do?' she cried, pulling away from him to stand by the table, arms tightly clasped around herself.

Alessandro took his time answering. 'I salvaged your reputation,' he drawled, with such barefaced arrogance that she was momentarily stunned.

'You salvaged *my* reputation by pretending that we have some sort of serious relationship that's actually going somewhere?' She laughed shortly, although her heart did a treacherous little flip inside her. She didn't want a serious relationship with him…*did she*? A fine film of perspiration broke out on her skin. This wasn't what this was about. This was about lust. Lust was simple. Anything more than that was a dangerous minefield.

'Did you really want my father to think that you were the sort of girl who would jump into bed with a guy just for the hell of it? You don't have to be a genius to see that my father's placed you on some sort of pedestal. I might have known that a lot sooner if we'd had the sort of father-son relationship where meaningful conversation played a part, but we didn't, so I never even knew of your existence until I came here. But as soon as I saw the interaction between the two of you, I knew that he…maybe looks on you as the daughter he once had.' Alessandro's voice was gruff and he began to prowl restlessly through the kitchen, pausing only to lean heavily on the counter by the kitchen sink, where he stared out of the window for a while at the acres of open fields and cultivated gardens outside, barely visible in the thickening snow.

'Did you…' he turned to face her '…really want me to shatter those illusions?'

'Maybe not, but to lead him on like that…'

'It's not a complete lie. We do have a relationship.'

'Of sorts, Alessandro. We have a relationship *of sorts*.' And she wasn't going to make the mistake of turning that into anything else. 'We have the sort of relationship that's going to fizzle out the minute you leave here and return to London. That's something we both knew from the very beginning.' She was proud of the way her voice was low but calm, urgent but composed.

'Let's get past the moral high ground,' he drawled with infuriating arrogance. 'There was also the issue of my father's health. He hasn't been a well man. I had several conversations with his consultant when he had his stroke a few months ago, and I was told that lack of stress was the safest route to ensuring that his health continued to improve.'

'That's rich, considering you came here to yank him away from everything he was accustomed to.'

Alessandro flushed darkly. 'When I decided to move him down to London, I wasn't aware of the extent of the ties he had built up in the community.'

Laura reddened because she knew that. Everything had been straightforward when he had made the decision to move Roberto. He could never have foreseen the way events would unfold.

'It's bad enough that your father thinks that we're involved but it's only going to be worse when he tells my grandmother. She spent so long clucking around me when

I returned to Scotland that she's going to think you're a knight in shining armour who's come swooping in to rescue me. I can't think of anyone less like a knight in shining armour,' she finished glumly, for good measure, missing the irritated frown that darkened his face.

'Well, here we are,' he said silkily. 'For better or for worse.'

'And where do we go from here?'

'Like I said to you earlier, let's just go with the flow.' He shot her a wicked smile, which she did her best to ignore, and walked slowly towards her. 'We may not end up walking up the aisle in happily married bliss but we're good together. Let's not think beyond that.' To prove his point, he touched her cheek and, with satisfaction, watched the way her eyelids fluttered. 'When the time comes, we break up and there will be no fuss. Relationships end, even those that begin with high hopes...so, until that happens, let's take this golden opportunity to enjoy one another.'

No strings attached...and no hiding... He made it sound so simple. So why, Laura wondered, did it feel so dangerous?

CHAPTER NINE

A PROPER HOLIDAY!

Roberto and Edith had confronted them an hour later and announced that that was what they should do. Despite the snow, *the serious relationship* had been compelling enough for Roberto to get in touch with his occasional driver, who had brought Edith to the manor house post-haste.

Laura had been horrified.

She was still reeling from the shock of Alessandro's deception and the ease with which he had accepted their fling as something that would now carry on until, presumably, he got fed up and decided to call it a day. He just went right ahead and assumed that the ball was in his court, that he called the shots, and now the way had been paved for the whole thing to cost him a lot less effort.

For Alessandro, fabricating a so-called serious relationship to appease his father made perfect sense. Indeed, it was an improvement on trying to figure out the details of how they could conduct a sexual liaison behind Roberto's back.

The situation had moved so swiftly that Laura felt as though she had inadvertently stepped onto a roller coaster and was now being swung in sickening circles hundreds of metres above the ground.

Her life had been so orderly before he had crash-landed

into it. She had been contentedly doing her teaching job and getting over her awful experience in London. The peace of Scotland had been a soothing balm for her fraught nerves and if she hadn't asked herself any questions about how long she could continue leading a life of relative contentment before restlessness began to set in, it was because she had chosen not to.

And then suddenly there he was, the missing son whom she had never seen, bringing with him just the sort of dark excitement she had sworn to stay well away from.

Worse—bringing the sort of dark excitement she had never dreamed possible. It overshadowed everything Colin had represented. He had turned those dark, lazy, arrogant eyes on her and her peaceful world had been shattered into smithereens.

It was so simple for him. He took what he wanted. Just the sort of guy she should have run from and kept on running from until she ran out of breath and found herself a nice little hole to hide in.

But what had she done instead? She had let those eyes settle on her, mesmerise her, get her thinking all sorts of things about the perfectly adequate life she had been content to lead.

Wasn't it better to live a little? To take a chance? Why fight the overwhelming attraction she felt for him? Why store up regret for missed opportunities? Why not get out of her comfort zone?

He had infected her with his cavalier way of thinking and she had yielded mindlessly.

She could control physical attraction, she had argued. If anything, it would do her good not to pigeonhole herself.

She'd never expected that she would become so entangled in his narrative to the extent that she lost track of her own.

And here she was now. Involved in a charade of a relationship for the benefit of her grandmother and his father. He might be able to take that in his stride but she wasn't fashioned from such stern stuff.

Guilt nagged at the edges of her consciousness and she surfaced to find that a long weekend was being planned around her. A cup of tea had found itself in her hand and she sipped some hurriedly as she tried to gather herself and focus.

'That house of yours!' Roberto was booming with authority. 'Made a big deal of it in the newspapers a few years ago! Bought with some of the petty cash from that oil-refinery deal of yours! Somewhere hot…escapes me where…'

'The Caribbean,' Alessandro filled in succinctly, amused and still startled at just how much information his father had gathered about him over the years. He looked at Laura, who was gulping down her tea as though her life depended on it.

'Bet you've never stepped foot in the place!' His father looked at him shrewdly and Alessandro decided on the spot that that was precisely where he would take her.

Why not?

He didn't like the way he couldn't stop thinking of her. He'd had enough upheavals of late without his work life suffering further because it was constantly being interrupted with visions of her in his arms, naked and spreading her legs, begging for him. He needed to get her out of his system, and once he'd done that he would allow a decent interval before letting slip that things, sadly, had not worked out. Life. What could you do?

In the meanwhile, a few days of uninterrupted sex should do the trick.

If she didn't decide to throw obstacles in the way, and from the look of her stubborn little mouth, he wasn't sure.

He banked down a spurt of irritation. 'It's been hard to find the time,' he murmured. 'Of course, it hasn't been entirely unused. I reward top employees with the occasional holiday there. But you know what? I think a few days' relaxation in the sun wouldn't be a bad idea...'

'But what about the house? The move? All the packing left to do?' Belatedly, she remembered that she was supposed to have found the love of her life, and she tempered her borderline refusal with a smile. 'Just saying...'

'Taking those objections in order,' Alessandro informed her comfortably, 'the house is progressing smoothly, the move is scheduled to take place within the next three weeks and as for the packing...well, we've covered the better part of anything too valuable for the removal men. Why don't we let my father and Edith take it from here? They may want to spend some time together without having us around as chaperones...'

'I'm not sure about clothes...stuff for warm weather...'

Alessandro shrugged his shoulders as though that particular objection wasn't worth answering. 'Don't tell me you only have a wardrobe of winter gear. I won't believe you.' He slanted her a smile of amused, indulgent warmth. 'It may rain and snow a lot in Scotland but summer still occurs once a year. Correct me if I'm wrong. Shorts and T-shirt weather? Anyway, there are one or two shops on the island, if memory serves me. I may not have been there for a couple of years but I distinctly remember them catering lavishly for the tourists. Leave tomorrow morning, return Sunday evening. What could be more relaxing?'

Laura thought that it might have been very relaxing if they weren't going to be labouring under a cloud of deception. As it stood, she could think of a million more relaxing ways of spending a weekend.

'Seems an awfully long way to go for just a few days...' She smiled weakly because Roberto and her grandmother were both staring at her as though she had taken leave of her senses. 'Jet lag, you know...'

'You're young!' Roberto barked, dismissing this half-hearted objection with a wave of his walking stick. 'Leave the complaints about jet lag to old fogies like Edith and myself! *We're* the ones who would suffer from jet lag after a long flight! Suffer from jet lag when I go to Edinburgh! Take yourself out there, my girl, and see a bit of the world! *You...*' he looked at Laura from under his bushy brows '...need to get out of here for a little while before you start fossilising...remember that you're still young! And *you...*' he looked at Alessandro '...need a break from that computer of yours! Not to mention that I could do without having you under my feet all the time! Everywhere I look you're there, nagging, nagging, nagging...'

Over the next twenty-four hours, Laura felt her panic level rise.

She no longer knew where she stood. Her grandmother had cornered her the second they were back at their house and had started making noises about engagements, marriage and babies. She had turned misty-eyed at the thought of a little great-granddaughter. Laura had been frankly appalled but had had to smile through the conversation while making sure to reveal as little as possible.

Yes, she could understand why Alessandro had said what he had said on the spur of the moment, but she still simmered with resentment because it was an added complication to a situation that had already been threatening to become complicated.

Involvement.

That was the dreaded word that hovered at the back of her mind like a nasty little thorn.

She had stupidly signed up for a bit of fun. She had conveniently overlooked the fact that she wasn't a *fun girl*. She was a serious girl who wanted love, security and commitment. And while she had enjoyed every second of Alessandro's raw physicality, she had also strayed into more dangerous territory, had allowed herself to become involved with him. She had done that because that was just *who she was*. Fighting her own nature would have been like trying to plug a leaking hole in a dam with sticky tape.

Which was why, now, waiting for him to collect her and take her to the airport, she just didn't know what she had got herself into.

Her grandmother had been fussing since dawn and had made her a little packed breakfast to take with her in the car. Or on the plane. She had been repeatedly given strict instructions about sunblock, even though Laura couldn't see how much damage could be done to her skin in the space of a couple of days. She had been warned several times about mosquitoes.

She heard the sharp ring of the doorbell and there was a flurry of goodbyes and then she was in the car with him. The snow had diminished overnight, but the fields were still thinly covered and the temperature was bitingly cold.

'It's not going to be a very enjoyable long weekend if you decide to give me the silent treatment,' Alessandro drawled, casting a sideways look at her. He startled her by pulling over to the side of the isolated road and killing the engine.

'What are you doing?'

'Getting our relaxing break off to a good start.'

Laura's eyes skittered over his potent, masculine body,

idly leaning against the car door as he looked at her. She felt a rush of pure sexual craving and wondered why on earth she couldn't just relax and enjoy the situation for what it was. After all, there wasn't anything she could do to change it.

And it wasn't as if they hadn't already made love. They had. He knew her body as intimately as she knew his.

'You're overanalysing. You're letting your mind run away with all sorts of erroneous detail because my father knows about us. So he knows. So he thinks that what we have is more than it actually is. That's an unalterable fact, but,' he said drily, 'let me make this very simple for you. I want you. You want me. And we're about to go abroad for three days of very hot sex.'

'You're very black and white.'

'I'm a pragmatist.' His lean face wore a wolfish expression. In one easy movement he leaned towards her and slowly raised her thick jumper, then the thermal long-sleeved vest underneath, until both were gathered above her breasts.

He was proving how simple sex was. She knew that and while her head was jammed with conflicting thoughts, she still couldn't resist the warm pressure of his hands as he reached behind to unclasp the bra so that her breasts spilled out, her nipples tightening at the drop in temperature.

He looked at them, dark eyes hot and appreciative.

'We...we should be going to the airport... We can't... Not here...'

'I'm not going to make love in this car,' Alessandro said, his eyes flicking to her heated face. 'Too small for a big man like me. No, I'm just going to do a little touching...' He leaned over to lick her nipples and she sank lower in the car seat. To watch his dark head suckling at her breasts with the bleak open fields stretching on either side was unbelievably erotic. Wetness seeped through her underwear but in the confined space she couldn't rub her legs together to relieve the ache there and he wasn't going to put her out of her torment by going any further than her breasts.

It was sweet torture and she was as helpless as a kitten as he continued to suck and tease her nipples. The only sounds were the sounds of his mouth on her, and then he stopped and neatly pulled down her bra, her vest and the jumper, and sat back.

'Enjoy what we have,' he said, starting the car and slowly pulling away from the grass verge to continue their journey. 'We are where we are. No need to get tense about it.'

Laura was busy doing up her bra, tidying herself and wondering how he could manage to prove a point with such consummate ease. How could she explain to him that she wasn't as black and white as he was, when she had gaily launched herself into a no-strings-attached affair, cheerfully accepting that it was going nowhere? What right did she have to suddenly start pulling moral scruples out of the bag? How hypocritical was that?

They were going by private jet. For such a short holiday, she was told that it worked. She listened and contributed to the conversation. She knew that she was asking all sorts of interested questions about a private jet—when he used it, didn't he think it was environmentally destructive?

'You'll have to get rid of all those thick clothes,' he drawled, as they boarded the sleek, black jet that was waiting for them on a private airstrip she had never known existed. For a while, Laura forgot every qualm and doubt.

This was what it felt like to step into something that reeked of money. It was travel without the hassle of an airport and the discomfort of crowds of people. He was amused as he stood back and watched her poke and pry,

scarcely hearing him when he told her that he had made
sure that a selection of light clothes be brought to the plane.
He guided her into a separate, private room with a relaxing sofa and indicated the neat stacks of clothes. He stood
by the door, glanced at his watch, eventually told her to
get a move on because they would be taking off shortly.

'I brought my own clothes.' Laura looked down at the
bright collection in front of her. Tropical colours. Colours
she would never have dreamed of wearing.

'So now you have more than you need. Isn't that every
woman's dream?'

'I've told you already that I'm not like every woman
so, no, that's never been a dream of mine.' She held up
one strappy, frothy little number and twirled it in front of
her with a frown.

'Try it, Laura,' Alessandro encouraged softly. 'Dare to
live a little… And I'll meet you outside in five minutes. I
need to make some urgent calls.'

Laura glared at his departing back. *Dare to live a little?*
It felt as though she had been doing nothing but *daring to
live a little*, for weeks and weeks and weeks. If she hadn't
been so *daring to live a little*, she wouldn't be here now,
with her thoughts in a dizzy whirl and an orange-and-pink
sundress in her hand!

She would be…safe.

And she didn't want to be safe. She wasn't sure whether
she would ever *want* to be *safe* again.

Because there was no excitement in a safe world. No
thrills, no lurching stomach, no heightened senses, no
edge-of-cliff feelings.

No Alessandro.

She sat down heavily on the sofa, her breath coming
and going in fast little pants. She stared, glassy-eyed, at
the dress in her hand and tried to arrange her thoughts in a

way that wouldn't point her in a direction she didn't want to follow, but she felt sick.

When had he become an integral part of her life? When had he stopped being someone she disapproved of and turned into someone who filled all the spaces in her head?

When had she fallen in love with him? How on earth could something as big as love happen so fast?

It was nothing like what she had felt for Colin. That had been a silly crush, born from her own insecurities and his persistent flattery.

Alessandro had seduced her with more than flattery. He had seduced her with his intelligence, his wit, his depth. She had lost her head and her heart to the way he looked at her, the way he smiled, the way he sometimes laughed. The way he had dealt with the upheaval in his life when his father had finally broken the ice and told him about his past. He hadn't played to her insecurities and taken advantage of them. He had dispelled them and shown her what it was to feel beautiful and sexy.

Was that why she had slept with him? Had her heart driven her to do what came naturally, even though her head had not yet had time to play catch-up? She had fooled herself into thinking that she was filling a physical need and hadn't looked deeper.

And this was why she felt so panicked and scared now. Because it was so much more than a fling, so much more than two people enjoying sex before it fizzled out.

She wasn't comfortable, not at all, with the idea of deception, with thinking that her grandmother and Roberto were harbouring the illusion that this was some kind of serious relationship, and she was downright terrified at the murky waters into which she had waded.

'Fallen asleep? Do you need your knight in shining

armour to come and administer some mouth-to-mouth resuscitation?'

Laura heard that deep, sexy drawl and changed out of her winter clothes into the sundress faster than the speed of light. There was a pale, silky cardigan amongst the bundle of clothes and she stuck that on.

'Shame.' Alessandro had spent the past couple of hours with an extremely painful erection and seeing her in a dress that could have been personally made to outline her curvaceous little body didn't help matters. 'I was looking forward to the mouth-to-mouth revival scenario…'

Laura smiled weakly. Now that she had recognised her feelings for what they were, everything about him seemed to affect her all the more powerfully. Draped in the doorway, he was so staggeringly beautiful that she could barely speak. He had stripped down to a T-shirt and his low-slung jeans, and he oozed shameful sexuality. When her eyes drifted south, she went bright red at the glaring proof of how she affected him.

His jeans bulged where a rampant erection sent her senses into a giddy tailspin.

'I know.' Alessandro followed the direction of her gaze and read her reaction with no trouble at all. 'But, sadly, we haven't got time. Although…I *could* tell the crew to—'

'No!' Laura yelped, as he made a move towards her. She remembered the way he had suckled her breasts at the side of the road, not at all fazed at the thought that someone might drive past them and figure out what was going on.

He was in charge of this situation because he wasn't emotionally involved.

She nipped past him and smoothed down the dress with shaky hands. 'It's not really my style at all.'

'You're a knockout in it, though…' He grinned because she might be as hot as a naked flame between the sheets, but out of them she was as skittish as a colt and still blushed like a teenager. 'And you'll be glad for it when we get to the other end. Baking hot.'

They were in their seats and he solicitously strapped her in, shooting her a wicked little look as his arm brushed against her breast.

'What do you think your crew thinks of *this*…of *us*…?'

'Don't know. Don't care.'

'Is there *anything* you really care about, Alessandro?' The sharpness of her tone was muffled by the roar of engines as the jet began taxiing to take off.

'There's a certain deal hanging by a thread.' His voice was amused but his night-dark eyes were cool. '*That's* getting my attention at the moment. I certainly care about *that*.'

'But there must be more to life than deals.'

'Are you about to start delivering a lecture on my life choices?' Alessandro asked smoothly, angling his big body to look at her. 'I immerse myself in what I know. Work. Business. Money. And when it comes to emotions, because I take it that's what you're talking about, I control them.' He raised both eyebrows and tilted his head to one side.

'By control, you mean you never allow yourself to really feel anything for anyone…'

'Since when have you had this interest in what I feel or don't feel and why?'

Laura blushed.

Since she had finally admitted to herself just how deeply she had fallen for him.

She shrugged. 'We all try to find out what makes other people tick. It's human nature.'

'Really? I have yet to want to find out how any woman ticks.' Except that wasn't quite true, was it? He closed his mind to a line of querulous introspection he had no use for.

Laura pasted a smile on her face. No big surprise there. He slept with women, just as he was sleeping with her, but that was the extent of his involvement. As he'd said, he exercised control over his emotions and the things in life that didn't require emotion were the things that garnered his dispassionate interest. Those were the things he wanted to pick apart and examine in detail.

That hurt and she hated that it hurt. When she was with him, she could feel all one hundred per cent of his fabulous interest focused on her and it stung to recognise that he would be the same in the company of any woman he wanted to bed.

She had fallen in love with a guy who had no interest in a future with her or with any woman. She was deceiving her grandmother and an old man she cared deeply for. On both scores she was behaving in a way that was completely against her nature. And now she was on a posh private jet off for a few days of complete seclusion with someone who was happy enough to promote a charade because it made life simpler all round for him. From every angle, she was vulnerable and she would have to at the very least try to curtail the fallout, and step one would be to make sure he didn't get wind of just how deeply he affected her.

She thought about his reaction if he were to discover that this was so much more than just a fling for her.

He would be appalled, horrified, aghast. Or maybe... amused, comfortable with the thought that he could call all the shots, knowing that she would oblige. He wouldn't see it as taking advantage of her. He would simply accept that she had fallen for him so that made her an easier conquest. He would exercise the instincts of the born predator. She wondered how many women had fallen in love with him in his chequered past.

'You've never been tempted to have something more than a superficial relationship with anyone?'

'Whoever said that my relationships were superficial?' Alessandro asked, not liking the way that somehow made him appear shallow. Which he wasn't. Simply practical, careful and controlled. 'I'm a red-blooded man. I enjoy women and when I'm with a woman I'm with her and no one else. Unlike, might I add, the creep you went out with. What sort of man would you prefer? A man who was up-front and honest or a man who was willing to say whatever he thought would get you between the sheets, even if he had no intention of fulfilling any of the promises he made? And I'm presuming the creep you dated was full of promises.'

Laura flushed because, yes, Colin had had the big gestures down pat along with the flowery words and the overblown promises. But, between the two, surely there was a happy medium, the place that most people occupied? Except that wouldn't be a place Alessandro would ever have occupied or even been tempted to explore.

She yawned and half closed her eyes because their conversation was going nowhere.

She didn't think she would be able to sleep at all, not when she was travelling in a private jet with a man she was in love with and a wasp's nest of uncomfortable thoughts buzzing around in her head, but, in fact, she slept soundly and only awoke when Alessandro nudged her and she opened her eyes to find him looking at her with amusement.

'It's unusual to have women fall asleep in my company,' he quipped, still smiling as the plane began its descent.

'I suppose they're too busy trying to impress you.' She struggled into a sitting position and transferred her eager eyes to the bright blue skies outside. Holiday excitement unfurled inside her and she shut the door on all the doubts that had been eating her up for the past few hours.

'They would have spent the better part of the trip trying to get me into the bed in the private room.'

'Idiots,' Laura said tersely. 'Would they be hoping that you might be interested enough with their antics to prolong the relationship?'

Alessandro was still smiling that smile that made her go all shivery and adolescent inside. 'Not a one-way street,' he countered smoothly. 'I'd like to think they'd get as much pleasure as they might be desperate to give. Angling for a committed relationship wouldn't have entered the equation.'

Laura didn't say anything. What was there to say? She directed her attention to the stunning vista now sprawling into view and gasped. She'd had no idea what to expect at the other end of the flight she had largely slept through. Her life had hardly been littered with holidays abroad. Growing up, she and her grandmother had been to France a couple of times and she had been to Spain with girlfriends a few years previously. While she had been working in London her holidays had consisted of returning to Scotland. She certainly had no experience of anywhere outside Europe and her stunned amazement at island life continued to keep her entranced as she followed in Alessandro's imperious wake until finally, with the sun beginning to set, they were heading off to his villa.

It was hot. She had to dispose of the thin cardigan as soon as she stepped foot out of the plane. And the sounds... The sounds of insects all around her, noisy but out of sight. She could smell the faint, salty tanginess of the sea. She began peppering him with all the questions she would have asked on the plane had she managed to keep her eyes open. It seemed that the island was very small, tiny, a little jewel in the sea where the rich and famous had houses that were nestled in lush, tropical grounds, far, far away from the prying eyes of the paparazzi. Tourism accounted for most of the income of the locals and the businesses that had sprung up on the island were there as a response to the millionaires and billionaires who had houses there, some of them permanently occupied rather than used now and again.

There was someone to meet them, a smiling, dark-skinned guy who chatted for the duration of the short trip, at the end of which the four-wheel-drive car bumped away from the main road and ascended an incline. On either side of the narrow road, trees and bushes vied to gain control. Tall coconut palms swayed above dense shrubs, and wildly colourful flowers dotted the undergrowth.

Laura feasted her eyes until the road gave way to a small courtyard in which stood a low, ranch-like house. Simply put, it was spectacular. A wooden porch spanned the length of it. She barely noticed the driver melting into the darkness, and inside the house she paused and looked around her, open-mouthed.

'How can you never come here?' she wondered aloud, and Alessandro shrugged.

'Time constraints. It's late. The place is fully stocked with food. I could have arranged with someone to come and cook while we're here, but I didn't see much point, considering we're only going to be here for a short while...' Her hair had fallen into wild ringlets. He had never set eyes on anything quite so disingenuously tempting. 'But shall we postpone the food until we've freshened up?' he murmured encouragingly, strolling towards her, wanting her to feast her eyes on *him* and not on her surroundings.

He hadn't been to this house for quite a while, but he could still recall its layout, and if memory served him right the bathroom adjoining the main bedroom was big enough and lavish enough to host a party. He looped his arms around her, turned her so that she was looking at him and lowered his head to kiss her.

'I want to explore the house first,' Laura breathed, and Alessandro groaned.

'It's a house. Some bedrooms, a few other rooms, a pool, some lawns. What's to explore? The only room I want you to explore is the bedroom.'

'It's not all about sex!' But the hot urgency of his voice filled her with a fierce longing that craved satisfaction. He occupied so much space in her head that just seeing the way his dark eyes were fastened on her made her want his hands and his mouth on her body. As easy as that, he could ignite all her senses.

It took all her willpower not to blindly let him lead her into the bedroom. Instead, they explored the house, which was beyond amazing.

There was, apparently, air conditioning throughout, but right now the house had been aired and as he flung open doors and shutters, balmy breezes blew in. The smell of the sea was even stronger here and he told her that it was a short walk down to a private cove. 'But not now,' he said drily, noticing the way she gazed wistfully through to the garden.

'It's just the most beautiful house.' She ran her eyes over the exquisite wooden flooring, gleaming through lack of use, and the light bamboo furniture and fine muslin drapes. 'Like from a magazine.'

'And I've saved the best for last,' Alessandro murmured, drawing her away from the living area towards the bedrooms, although he'd already made his mind up, and individual see-and-touch exploring sessions within the seven guest ones wasn't going to happen. At least not right now, when his libido was making walking a challenge.

The master bedroom, reserved for his exclusive use, was at the far end of the house and opened out, through French doors, to a view of the ocean. It had its own private veranda and he watched as she took it all in with open awe. He had flung open the French doors and she stepped outside to breathe in the clean, warm tropical air. Then she admired the giant bed with its gauze curtains, which would have seemed feminine were it not for the dark-coloured bedding and the starkness of the furnishings.

Without even noticing, she only realised that she had been led by the hand into the biggest bathroom she had ever seen when he began tugging the strap of her sundress.

Laura gazed up at him helplessly. It mystified her that she couldn't create some distance between them when she knew that this was a situation that was going to leave her stranded and hurt. There was not one single part of her that could resist when he touched her, even when he glanced at her. She burned for him and made absolutely no attempt to stop him from undressing her. The sundress was tugged down, pooling at her feet, and she obediently stepped out of it, then off came the bra and the knickers so that she was standing naked in the vast bathroom while he was still fully clothed.

It was unreasonably erotic but when she reached to strip him of his shirt, he stilled her hand with a half-smile.

'I need to go slowly,' he breathed huskily. 'Watching you sleep on the plane tested me to the outer limits. If we have sex right now, I won't be able to do justice to the act.'

Pink tinged her cheeks and she reached up as he began kissing her, very slowly and very thoroughly, and as he kissed her he played with her breasts, murmured into her ear, told her things that made her face burn and turned her on so much she could barely contain the feverish excitement coursing through her body.

He eased himself lower until he was kneeling before her. Laura could scarcely stand. Her legs felt like jelly because she was so turned on, and the hand that gently slipped between her thighs to part her legs elicited a moan in response.

Legs apart, she flung back her head and savoured the exquisite sensation of his tongue probing the wet slit, slipping between the folds of her femininity to tickle the roused bud of her clitoris. Of their own accord, her fingers curled into his hair. She widened her stance, created more space for his lazy exploration, sank into the caress of his wet mouth between her legs.

Her orgasm came fast and furious, building quickly and carrying her away with a whoosh.

A sultry breeze blew through the open window. So alien from what she was used to. Even the loud, shuddering groan that escaped her lips didn't seem to come from her. Neither, she thought, opening drowsing eyes and catching sight of herself in the mirrored wall opposite, did this woman resemble the one she thought she was and always had been.

She was in a parallel universe and all she could do was wait for the bump when she returned to earth to happen…

That…and protect herself the best she could…

CHAPTER TEN

SITTING BY THE infinity pool, slowly being toasted by the sun, which was still hot even though it was after five in the afternoon, Laura reflected that time had stood still and now the hands of the clock were once more on the move.

First thing the following morning the private jet that had whisked them to his island paradise would be whisking them away from it and back to reality. Harsh, inescapable reality.

They hadn't spoken once about the so-called relationship they were supposed to have, concocted for the sake of his father and her grandmother. They were supposed to be madly in love. They were supposed to be thinking about a series of *tomorrows* and not just the here and now, but that was just a technicality that suited Alessandro. He'd told her to forget about Roberto and her grandmother and to see the long weekend as an opportunity for hot sex, and such was his hold over her heart that she had pushed her anxieties and misgivings to one side and, yes, coward that she was, she had enjoyed him. Enjoyed him, being with him and the glorious tropical paradise into which she had landed. A little sparrow thrown into an exotic world far beyond her reach.

She couldn't have been further out of her comfort zone. The little island was the playground of the fabulously wealthy. Vast plantation-style houses were screened behind sweeping, palm-tree-lined drives. Exquisite beaches were nestled into the mountains, although they had actually been to only one of those because they had their own beach, a beach with sand as fine and as white as icing sugar with placid, turquoise water to swim in. The town centre was picturesque, with several top-rated restaurants, a few very expensive shops and then all the other businesses that were needed to support the economy of the island and keep the locals employed.

She had felt as though she had inadvertently stepped onto a movie set. Everything was so picture-perfect that there was an air of unreality about the experience.

It was as unreal as their relationship and she knew that being on this island was like being in a bubble, where it was easy to forget about things that would need to be dealt with.

She sighed and shut her eyes. When she opened them, it was to see Alessandro standing by the sun lounger, looking at her through sunglasses.

'You're not the picture of joy and rapture,' he said without preamble.

Laura shielded her eyes against the glare of the sun and propped herself up on her elbow. Would she ever tire of the sight of him? He took her breath away. When he was near, her heart beat faster and her pulse raced. There was no bit of her, emotionally, physically, intellectually, into which he didn't intrude. He had managed to take over her entire being and when she thought about him no longer being around she felt as though she was staring into a black, bottomless void that filled her with tearing emptiness and despair.

She knew that she had only herself to blame. He hadn't asked her to fall in love with him. In fact, he had made it clear from the start that love was a four-letter word that didn't exist in his vocabulary. If her heart had broken free of its leash, that had had nothing to do with him.

'I'm going to miss all this when we leave...' She forced a smile as he settled into the sun lounger next to her.

His first thought was that the house wasn't going anywhere. Who was to say that she wouldn't be back? Then he frowned because that was just the sort of forward planning he always avoided with a woman.

'Holidays in the sun aren't out of reach just because you live in Scotland.' He shrugged and Laura kept on smiling because that was just the sort of response she didn't want. Of course he couldn't guess that a *holiday in the sun*, any old *holiday in the sun*, wasn't what she was talking about.

'I'll have to start saving,' she said lightly. 'Believe it or not, teachers don't earn all that much...'

Alessandro slanted a killer smile and leaned on his side, feathering a light touch on her arm and feeling the soft shudder of her body with a familiar, mounting arousal. She was so responsive and that never failed to turn him on. He couldn't get enough of her. 'I admit this particular resort is probably out of reach for the average teacher,' he murmured, 'unless, of course, the average teacher happens to be the lover of the above-average tycoon... I'm glad you enjoyed it here. It's good for the place to get a little use.'

'Why do you have places like this if you never use them?'

'As investments,' Alessandro said lazily. 'It's not exactly killing me. This house has appreciated substantially in value since it was bought and right now I'm glad I was never tempted to sell it.'

'So you've never brought anyone here?'

'When you say *anyone*...'

'Women. Those lucky women who you happened to be dating...'

'I've tended to stick closer to home.'

'Why's that?'

'I really want you right now...'

'When you don't want to talk, you resort to the physical. I've noticed that.'

Alessandro flung himself back and stared up at the bright blue sky. He'd never known a woman more disrespectful of his boundaries. He pointed them out, she saw them and then she proceeded to trample all over them as though they didn't exist.

'I happen to enjoy the physical,' he said, turning to her, and she looked at him with something approaching pity. 'It beats,' he was pressed to continue irritably, 'having long, meaningful conversations about things that don't matter.'

Laura's soft mouth tightened. 'Well...I hate to burst your bubble but sometimes people do have to have long, meaningful conversations, even if you find them boring and irrelevant.'

She hadn't meant to have this conversation. It cast a stormy cloud over what remained of the little paradise she had spent the past few days occupying, but how could she carry on pretending? Knowing that the more time she spent with him, the deeper in love she fell and the more painful it would eventually be to extricate herself?

What a mess.

Alessandro stilled. Did he want to hear this? He sat up and removed his sunglasses to look at her.

Laura's heart was racing. Her mouth was dry. Did she really want to ruin what was left of their stay here? She could laugh and change the subject. She could just accept that it wasn't an ideal situation but why rock the boat, why not just enjoy what was on offer until the offer was rescinded? Why not play the game, as he suggested, and when things ended, just explain to Roberto and her grandmother that it hadn't worked out in the end? Why not enjoy the hedonistic pleasure they got from one another and enjoy it without an agonising guilty conscience?

But how much enjoyment would she honestly get, knowing that it was just a matter of time before everything came crashing down around her and she was left to pick up the pieces? Every time he touched her, she would think that it might be the last. Every time she gazed at him, she would have to try not to let her feelings show, knowing that if he suspected the depth of what she felt, he would run a mile.

It would be like walking in a field of flowers knowing that underneath the perfect ground a series of landmines was waiting to be detonated.

'I never said that I found them boring or irrelevant,' Alessandro said carefully.

'I can't play this game. I can't just have a mindless affair with you. I can't take advantage of what my grandmother and Roberto mistakenly assume to have no-strings-attached sex. That's just not the way I'm made.' Her eyes shot away from his lean, beautiful face. 'I know you think it's a straightforward situation, I know you think that it makes it easier for us to…well, have this fling and then, when it comes to an end, we just break the news and walk away, but I…I can't do that.'

'Why not?' Alessandro demanded.

He knew. He raked restless fingers through his dark hair and stood up abruptly. The open space around him felt too small, pressing down on him. For the first time in his life the job of ridding himself of a woman who had made the terminal mistake of falling in love with him felt like an anchor dragging him down. And she did love him. He'd managed to shove that into his blind spot but she loved him.

He had his rules. He always made them clear. It had always been easy to bid farewell to someone who hadn't taken them on board. But then again, his boredom threshold was low. He had never felt the need to pursue any woman who wanted more than he was prepared to give. On the few occasions when this situation had presented itself, he had already been on the way to finding the whole thing pretty tedious anyway. Ending it had never been a hardship.

Not so now. He wasn't ready.

'Aside from the fact that I don't feel comfortable deceiving Roberto and Gran—'

'How are we being deceptive?' He spread his hands in a gesture of frustration. 'We have a relationship!'

'We don't have the sort of relationship they imagine we do.'

'We're not hurting anyone,' Alessandro persisted, bemused by his own inability to start the process of disentanglement and not wanting to voice the reality lying like a leaden weight between them. Their eyes tangled and he flushed darkly.

'Why don't you just say what you have to say and get it over and done with?' he rasped.

Laura hesitated, torn between a desperate need to try to patch things over and a driving urge to just tell him how she felt. She knew there was still a part of her that half hoped an admission of love wouldn't drive him away, and feeling like that, hoping against reason, annoyed and dismayed her.

She drew in a deep breath and held his gaze levelly, even though she was quaking inside.

'I'm too involved with you emotionally to do this, Alessandro,' she said, choosing her words carefully. 'It's not a game for me and if I carry on with...with *this*, I'm going to end up horribly hurt, and I don't want to be hurt.'

'I warned you not to...get involved. I told you I don't do love.'

'Sorry if I disobeyed orders!' Laura's voice had risen angrily. How could he just stand there and look at her as though she had suddenly turned into a stranger? His dark eyes were guarded and cool. 'Some of us actually have emotions!'

'I have emotions. I just know how to control them!'

'I can't do this.' She stood up and stormed off.

Alessandro watched her go but he had to force himself not to follow her. He waited until she was out of sight, unnerved by his indecision, and finally he swung round angrily and headed for the beach.

The sound of the sea would soothe him. He needed perspective but for the first time in his life perspective eluded him. She loved him and he had known and he hadn't walked away. Shouldn't that have been his first instinctive response?

He barely saw the picture-perfect-postcard beauty of the little cove, the clear water lapping at the shore, the backdrop of rocks and coconut palms. He barely felt the warmth pressing against him. He sat down, his back against one of the rocks, oblivious to everything but the swirling confusion of his thoughts.

She had breached his boundaries and no one could accuse him of not making those boundaries perfectly clear. She had strayed into no man's land.

And he had known. Deep down, he had known and he had basked in what she was giving him. And now that she had done the unthinkable and confirmed his suspicions, now that she had exposed the heart she had been wearing on her sleeve...

He raked his fingers through his hair, stood up, sat back down, glared at the perfect scenery.

How could he still want her? Why did the thought of her walking away fill him with fear and panic? Everything in his life had been so clear-cut before...*especially relationships...*

Why was the way forward so hard to see now? When he thought of her vanishing from his life, he felt...*empty.* It was as if a wilderness of trees had dropped down, obscuring the clear, open horizons of his life, and he just didn't know how to get past them. He could turn a full circle, and he still wouldn't be able to see past them to the life he'd had before.

With a low growl of bewilderment, frustration and inner turmoil, he strode out to the sea, dropping clothes en route, and took to the water.

Laura wanted him to follow her so badly that it was a physical ache in the pit of her stomach. Pride compelled her not to look round. She packed furiously, chucking her clothes into her bag while listening for the sound of his footsteps, and the longer the house remained silent, the more she held back the tears.

By eight, after a light snack, she resigned herself to the fact that he just wasn't going to follow her. There was no more talking to be done. In fact, she had no idea where he had gone and she refused point-blank to go out searching for him.

Even though worry clenched at her stomach when nine o'clock rolled round and there was still no sign of him.

For the first time since they had arrived, she fell asleep in the bed alone. At some point during the night she half heard him return and her whole body stiffened at the thought of him sliding into bed with her.

She longed for him but she knew that she had had no option but to be open and truthful.

Even though the consequences were beyond endurance.

He didn't sleep next to her. She heard the soft sound of him rustling and then he left the room.

The silence between them the following day was oppressive. When he addressed her it was with the politeness of a complete stranger and she heard herself responding in the same frozen voice, making sure to avoid eye contact, making sure to keep her distance. On the plane, she buried herself in her book while he sat in front of his computer, working.

They had nothing more to say and she was miserable.

They landed back in wintry weather and grey skies. Snow blanketed the ground and reflected her mood. The bright blue, tropical skies were gone for good. Next to her, Alessandro had spent most of the drive on the telephone. One call after another, catching up on work. After wearing nothing but the bright summer wear he had provided for her, she felt weighed down in her thick clothes.

'You don't have to deliver me back home.' She broke the silence to glance across at him.

'How do you suggest you get back?' Alessandro enquired. 'Do you plan on walking from my house back to your grandmother's with your suitcase on your back?'

'I don't want us to finish like this,' she said shakily. 'We could still…you know…remain friends…'

'That's not my style.' He'd been dumped. For the best because the last thing he needed was the complication of someone falling in love with him, someone expecting him to be the kind of man who was willing or, for that matter, *capable* of sharing himself. But he couldn't rid himself of the bitter, sour taste in his mouth. He'd spent hours the evening before walking on the beach, sitting and staring out at the black ocean in a foul mood, and things had not got better since.

Even more infuriating was the fact that he still wanted her. She had sat on the plane, absorbed in some book, oblivious to him, having dropped her little bombshell, and he had *still wanted her*.

He wasn't used to being dumped and he wasn't used to being ignored.

And now she talked about *being friends*?

'Fine,' Laura said stiffly. 'Don't say that I'm not trying to make peace between us.'

Alessandro's mood worsened. 'I take it your grandmother's expecting you?' he said curtly.

'I texted when I'd be back. Look, it's going to be very awkward if we walk in like enemies…'

'Well, now, maybe you should have considered that before…' He slid his eyes sideways. 'And how do you intend to break the news?'

'I'll just say that spending a long weekend together demonstrated that we didn't get along.'

'Which is a bald lie, isn't it?'

'I'm not prepared to keep something going for the sake of other people, not when it's a lie.' She sighed and looked at his harsh, averted profile. 'If I'd known… I…well, I never meant to get so wrapped up…'

He could never fall in love. He had built his entire life ruling out something he saw as a weakness. It was all she could do to stop herself from crying.

It was beginning to sleet by the time they made it to her grandmother's house. 'You don't have to see me in.' She turned to him as he killed the engine and sprawled back in the seat to look at her. 'It'll be easier if I go in alone and sit her down, break the news. You can…fill your dad in…'

'And then when we next meet we…what, exactly? Pretend we haven't been lovers? Going to be hard when you're in love with me and would like nothing better than to find the nearest bed, wouldn't you say?'

'Then I'll make sure to stay away until you're gone,' Laura said sharply. She opened the car door, bracing herself for the freezing cold, and was alarmed when he stormed out of his side, reaching to take her case to the front door.

He rang the doorbell, ignoring her as she scrambled to catch up to him. What the heck was he up to?

'You don't get to disappear,' he growled. They stared at one another. Unfair as it was, she couldn't tear her eyes away from his beautiful face.

She knew he was going to kiss her. She could read the intent in his dark eyes, but she was nailed to the spot and when his mouth met hers she whimpered and clutched the lapels of his coat. Oh, God, he tasted so sweet. *What was she doing?* Drowning. She was drowning and she hated herself for it but she couldn't seem to surface for life-giving air.

She was hardly aware of the door opening but when she was, she sprang back, her whole body trembling as she met her grandmother's eyes.

'This isn't what it looks like!' She looked at Alessandro, who was staring at her, not saying a word, making her wonder whether he had manoeuvred this situation just to make things difficult for her…because he still wanted her and wasn't ready to let her go.

Would he do that?

She could have slapped him.

'Roberto's here!' Edith chirruped, ushering them in, and so he was, along with another man whom Laura recognised, with a sickening jolt, as the local vicar. What on earth was he doing here? Somewhere between entering the house and finding themselves standing in the sitting room, Alessandro had taken her hand, linking her fingers through his.

Words tumbled over her head. The vicar just happened to be passing by...dropped in for a cup of coffee...was keen to meet the lovebirds...there was nothing more fulfilling than marriage...so many young people choosing to live together...but what a sight for sore eyes they both made...not meaning to presume but he would be honoured should they decide...

Laura tried and failed to meet Alessandro's eyes. Was he as shocked as she was? He seemed to be carrying the conversation, laughing and chatting and being horribly, horribly friendly, while she remained in mute silence, barely taking anything in until, after half an hour, she and Alessandro somehow found themselves alone in the sitting room.

'What just happened there?' Laura whispered. Alessandro had moved to stand by the fireplace and she looked at him, still reeling from the shock of having a future arranged on their behalves while Roberto and her grandmother had looked on contentedly.

'What did you expect me to do?' he asked fiercely. 'I was as surprised as you were.'

'Why didn't you say anything?'

'Why didn't you?'

'I was too dazed. I barely knew what was going on. Gran never mentioned a word... I can't believe Father Frank just happened to be passing by. What do we do now?' she half wailed and was taken aback when he continued to look at her without saying anything. He always knew what to say! Why was he just staring?

'It's not such a bad thing,' he muttered, and Laura's mouth fell open.

'Is that *all* you have to say? What the heck does that mean anyway?'

Alessandro raked unsteady fingers through his hair and

circled the room, finally coming to rest directly in front of her, a towering, brooding alpha male who, for once, was not his usual composed self. 'I'm not ready to…end what we have…'

'You're not ready to end what we have?' She laughed shortly. 'You don't give a damn about anyone but yourself, do you?' she demanded. 'You don't care how messed up I am, being an idiot to fall for you. You don't care that you've put me in an impossible situation. Just so long as you get what you want.' Tears pricked the backs of her eyes and she couldn't look at him. When she stared down, her fingers were restively curling and uncurling on her lap.

'You don't understand,' he muttered.

'Then why don't you explain? Tell me what it is I don't understand.'

'You make my world feel alive. When I'm with you, I feel as though my life makes sense.'

Laura's eyes fluttered. She didn't want to hope. Was this some kind of trick? Was she dreaming? Disoriented, she watched as he dragged a chair to sit next to her and for a few moments hung his head in a gesture that was so unlike him that she was worried. She tentatively laid her hand on his arm and without looking at her he blindly clutched it and held it tightly.

'You told me that you didn't expect to fall in love with me,' he said so quietly that she had to strain to hear. He raised his eyes and held hers. 'I rejected that. It was an automatic reaction. I always had my rules. No love, no commitment. No getting any ideas of permanence, but I hated the thought of not having you around. I hated it when we stopped talking to one another.'

'You hated not being able to carry on having sex with me because I haven't got past my sell-by date yet,' Laura persisted stubbornly.

'This is about more than just sex.'

'Strange you never mentioned that before, when I laid my soul bare. Strange all you did was disappear for hours and then sleep in a separate room! Where did you go anyway?'

'Are you jealous?'

'Oh, forget it!'

'I sat on the beach and looked at the sky and did some thinking.'

'And that's when you decided that you'd keep me on at all costs because you weren't sick of me quite yet?'

'I told myself that it was a good thing to finish it because I couldn't handle the expectations of any woman being in love with me.' He sighed heavily and pressed his thumbs over his eyes, then he looked at her. 'It never occurred to me that I only started asking myself why I didn't want what other people seemed to want when I met you. You made me question my pattern of behaviour. I grew up alone. I always saw that as a strength. To become emotionally involved with a woman would be to lose that strength and I never wanted to do that. But...'

'But...?' Laura pressed, her heart beating so hard she felt it might just burst out of her chest.

'But...I began to find out about my father, about myself. I began sharing myself with you in a thousand small ways and I didn't even realise I was doing it. I thought it was all about sex because that was how I had programmed myself to think, but it wasn't and today, driving back here...'

Laura held her breath, afraid to hope because it was impossible to second-guess this wonderful, complex, utterly fascinating man.

'I was scared,' he admitted, his amazing cheekbones tinged with a dark flush.

Something inside her melted. *He was scared.* That was

the most telling thing he had ever said to her and, looking at him, she believed him.

'Are you telling the truth?' she was still forced to ask, and he smiled crookedly at her.

'Lies are something I don't do as well. I'm telling the truth. I couldn't see a future unless you were in it and I knew that that must be love. What else? I'd never felt this way before. I barely recognised the signs and it was only now that it all made sense. I love you. I don't just want you. I need you and I love you and I can't stand the thought of you not being next to me every day for the rest of my life. Are you going to say anything? Or are you going to let me ramble on?'

'I'm keen to let you ramble on,' Laura whispered, and he grinned.

'I wasn't shaken by seeing the vicar here,' he said simply. 'I was glad. I was overjoyed because I want to do precisely what he and my father and your grandmother want us to do. I want to marry you. So...will you, Laura Reid, be my wife?'

And she smiled. *He loved her!* She wanted to fling her arms around him and shout from the rooftops at the same time.

'I love you so much, Alessandro,' she said instead, tracing the fabulous contours of his face with trembling fingers. 'You're my whole world and, yes, I'll marry you. You may have spent your life avoiding commitment but I'm warning you, you'll have a life sentence with me...'

'I can't think of anything I'd rather have more...'

'You see, there we have the crunch of the matter.'

* * * * *

9915_ST19

MILLS & BOON®
The Italians Collection!

2 BOOKS FREE!

Irresistibly Hot Italians

You'll soon be dreaming of Italy with this scorching six-book collection. Each book is filled with three seductive stories full of sexy Italian men! Plus, if you order the collection today, you'll receive two books free!

This offer is just too good to miss!

Order your complete collection today at
www.millsandboon.co.uk/italians

0715_ST16

MILLS & BOON®

Want to get more from Mills & Boon?

Here's what's available to you if you join the exclusive **Mills & Boon eBook Club** today:

✦ *Convenience – choose your books each month*
✦ *Exclusive – receive your books a month before anywhere else*
✦ *Flexibility – change your subscription at any time*
✦ *Variety – gain access to eBook-only series*
✦ *Value – subscriptions from just £3.99 a month*

So visit **www.millsandboon.co.uk/esubs** today to be a part of this exclusive eBook Club!